you're the one that I want

a gossip girl novel

Gossip Girl novels by Cecily von Ziegesar:

Gossip Girl
You Know You Love Me
All I Want Is Everything
Because I'm Worth It
I Like It Like That
You're the One That I Want

you're the one that I want

a gossip girl
novel

by
Cecily von Ziegesar

LITTLE, BROWN AND COMPANY
New York ✢ Boston

Little, Brown and Company

Time Warner Book Group
1271 Avenue of the Americas, New York, NY 10020
Visit our Web site at www.lb-teens.com

First Edition

Produced by 17th Street Productions,
an Alloy company
151 West 26th Street, New York, NY 10001

ISBN 0-316-73516-7

10 9 8 7 6 5 4 3 2 1
CWO
Printed in the United States of America

And if love is, what thing and which is he? If love be good, from whennes cometh my woo?

—Geoffrey Chaucer, *Troilus and Criseyde*

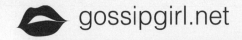 gossipgirl.net

Disclaimer: All the real names of places, people, and events have been altered or abbreviated to protect the innocent. Namely, me.

hey people!

You know the saying, Today is the first day of the rest of your life? I always thought that sounded so lame and corny, but today it actually seems sort of profound. Plus, I'm beginning to think there's nothing wrong with corny. It's okay to tell the doorman to have a good day when he opens the door for you in the morning on the way to school. And why not stop to smell the lilacs planted outside the apartment buildings along Fifth Avenue? While you're at it, go ahead and stick a bunch behind your ear. It's still only April, but you now have permission to wear those new mint green leather Coach flip-flops—you know, the ones with the little yellow roses embroidered on them that you've been wearing around the house for over a month?—*outside*. Of course you'll probably get into trouble at school for being out of uniform, but how else are you going to show off your new Brazilian pedicure?

I know, I know. You probably think I'm crazy to sound so upbeat since this is the week we all find out whether or not we were accepted at the colleges we applied to. It's the most critical thing that's happened to us thus far. From now on we'll be branded by the school we choose, or rather, the school that chooses us: the smarty-pants who got into Yale, the lesbionic B-student volleyball player bound for Smith, the flaky heiress whose dad bought her into Brown. All I'm saying is, why not look on the bright side? The letters are in the mail, what's done is done, and I for one am eager to move on.

That stupid game we all used to play (and secretly still do)

With college admissions almost behind us, now's the time to devote our full attention to something equally important: *our love lives*. It's about time you and the boy of your dreams (please add the line "in bed" to each of the following):

Drank Fuzzy Navels and stayed up until dawn

Fed each other hot fudge sundaes

Watched old movies

Went skinny-dipping

Blew smoke rings

Played Twister

Gave each other temporary tattoos

Named your children

Cut gym

Tried Bikram yoga

Not that I'm advocating anything too illegal. Now is definitely not the time to screw up. You heard about that promising young actress who got into Harvard last year and then ran off to LA to hang out with her actor boyfriend for the month of May? Harvard acceptance . . . revoked!! The above list is simply the best way I know of to shed the pounds of stress that have been weighing us down. Talk about a diet I might actually stick to!

Your e-mail

Dear Gossip Girl,
I just wanted to thank you for keeping my spirits up when I'm a total basket case. I don't know about you, but I applied to twelve schools and last night I dreamt I didn't get into one. Any advice on why I shouldn't run away to Mexico? Ur2cool.
—rose

Dear rose,
Mexico sounds good, but twelve schools? Come on, you're bound to get into one, or even all twelve! And in case you feel like hurling yourself off a bridge before all twelve letters turn up,

stick close to your friends . . . unless you're worried they might actually push you! This is a sensitive time for all of us.
—GG

Dear GG,
So is that crazy drug rehab girl from Connecticut, like, gone from **N**'s life? Because if he's single, I'm totally going to jump him.
—reddy

Dear reddy,
Sorry, honey, but you'll have to wait in line—and no cutting, please! Unfortunately for us, someone got to him first. Actually, she's always been there and probably always will be. I think you know who I'm talking about. But don't be too jealous: her life is anything but perfect.
—GG

Sightings

N waking and baking on the **Met** steps. I guess now that he's lax captain and is no longer hanging out with that fabulously insane drug rehab convict, he can relax and enjoy himself. **B** cutting assembly this morning to run home, on the off chance **Yale** was so eager to accept her they FedExed the letter for morning delivery. Talk about a basket case! **B** was also seen in **Barneys'** lingerie department trying on what can only be described as a "get lucky" ensemble. **S** biting her nails as she lay sunbathing in **Sheep Meadow** while scores of admiring boys looked on. What's she so worried about, anyway? **D** and **V** pretending not to notice each other as they waited on line to buy tickets to the new Ken Mogul film at the **Angelika**. **J** trying on a pair of wait-list-only python skin **Manolos** in **Bergdorf Goodman**. How exactly was she planning to pay for them, and where exactly is she planning to wear them? She may only be a freshman, but she's definitely ambitious.

Just in case you want to relive these precious moments . . .

V is making a documentary film about the whole getting-into-college thing. Think of it as an opportunity to vent and get four minutes in the limelight. For the next two weeks, she'll be filming near Bethesda Fountain in Central Park after school.

My fingers and toes are all crossed. Good luck, everybody!

You know I mean it,

gossip girl

b is the star of her own little movie

"Just talk about how you're feeling right now. You know, with college admission letters coming this week and everything." Vanessa Abrams squinted into the camera and adjusted the lens so Blair's jade-and-Swarovski-crystal chandelier earrings were in the frame. It was a balmy April afternoon and the park was a madhouse. Behind them a group of senior boys from St. Jude's chased a Frisbee up the terraced steps overlooking Bethesda Fountain, swearing and tackling one another in a frenzy of pent-up pre-college-admission stress. Around the perimeter of the fountain lay sprawled the perfectly tanned and manicured bodies of Upper East Side high-school girls, smoking cigarettes and rubbing their legs with the latest Lancôme tan invigorator, while the winged bronze lady in the center of the fountain gazed down on them forgivingly.

Vanessa pressed record. "You can start anytime."

Blair Waldorf licked her glossy lips and tucked the grown-out wisps of her dark brown pixie cut behind her ears. Underneath her plain black Polo shirt and gray Constance Billard uniform she was wearing the new turquoise-silk-and-black-lace underwire bra-and-thong set she'd bought in Barneys' lingerie department. She pressed her back against the fountain's rim and adjusted her butt on the folded-up bath towel Vanessa had given her to sit on.

Hot weather and thongs are a bad combination.

"I promised myself that if I got into Yale, Nate and I would finally do it," Blair began. She glanced down and twirled her ruby ring around and around on the ring finger of her left hand. "We're not even really together—*yet*. But we both know we want to be, and as soon as that letter comes . . ." She looked up at the camera, ignoring Vanessa's weirdly intense, shaven-headed, black-combat-boots-wearing stare. "For me it's not just about having sex, though. It's about my whole future. Yale and Nate. The two things I've always wanted."

She cocked her head. Actually, she wanted a lot of things. But except for that exquisite pair of Christian Louboutin silver lizard platform sandals, those were the two major ones.

"Nice try, loser!" a boy shouted as he snatched a Frisbee out of the air from under his friend's nose.

Blair closed her blue eyes and opened them again. "And if I *don't* get in . . ." She paused dramatically. "Someone is going to fucking pay."

Maybe she should be required to wear a muzzle this week.

Blair sighed, reached into her shirt, and adjusted her bra straps. "Some of my other friends—like Serena and Nate—aren't as freaked out about the whole college thing. But that's because they aren't living with their way-too-old-to-be-pregnant mom and their fat, gross stepfather. I mean, I don't even have my own room anymore!" She swiped a tear away and looked up at the camera with a mournful expression. "This is like my *one* chance to be happy. And I think I deserve it, you know?"

Cue applause.

n just wants to taste her lip gloss

Reaching the end of the elm-tree-lined promenade leading up to the Bethesda Terrace and Fountain, Nate Archibald tossed the nub end of the joint he'd been smoking to the ground and walked straight past his Frisbee-playing friends. Not ten feet away, Blair sat cross-legged at the base of the fountain, talking into a camera. She looked nervous and sort of innocent. Her delicate hands fluttered around her small, foxlike face, and her short gray school uniform barely covered her muscular thighs. He shook the golden brown locks out of his emerald green eyes and shoved his hands into his khaki pants pockets. She was sexy all right.

Of course, at that very moment every single female in the park was thinking exactly the same thing—about *him*.

Nate recognized the odd, shaven-headed girl behind the camera only vaguely. Normally Blair would have nothing to do with her, but she was always up for anything that involved talking about herself. Blair liked attention, and even after breaking up with her and cheating on her for the umpteenth time, Nate still liked giving it to her. He dipped his hand into the fountain, walked up behind her, and flicked a few drops of water on her bare arm.

Blair whipped her head around to find Nate looking irresistible as ever in a pale yellow button-down, unbuttoned, untucked, and rolled up, so all she could see were his wonderful tanned muscles and perfect face. "You weren't listening to what I said, were you?" she demanded.

He shook his head and she got up from the towel, ignoring Vanessa completely. As far as Blair was concerned, they were finished.

"Hey." Nate ducked down and kissed her cheek. He smelled like smoke and clean laundry and new leather—all the good boy smells.

Yum.

"Hello." Blair tugged on her uniform. Why the hell hadn't she gotten into Yale *today*?

"I was just thinking about how last summer you were completely addicted to ice cream sandwiches," Nate observed. He had a sudden urge to lick all that candy-sweet-smelling lip gloss off her lips and run his tongue over her teeth.

She pretended to adjust her new earrings so he would notice them. "I'm too nervous to eat, but lemonade would taste really good right now."

Nate smiled and Blair tucked her hand into the crook of his arm, just as she always used to when they went around together. The old familiar thrill passed through her. It was always like this when they got back together—comfortable and thrilling at the same time. They walked over to the vendor parked at the top of the steps and Nate bought two cans of Country Time lemonade. Then they sat down on a nearby bench and he removed a silver flask from his olive green canvas Jack Spade backpack.

Cocktail hour!

Blair ignored the lemonade and grabbed the flask.

"I don't know why you're nervous," Nate assured her. "You're like the best student in your class." Nate felt sort of ambivalent about getting into college. He'd applied to five schools and yeah, he wanted to get into one of them, but he was pretty confident he'd have a decent time wherever he went.

Blair took another swig from the flask before giving it back. "In case you forgot, I kind of totally fucked up *both* of my interviews?" she reminded him.

Nate had heard about her little nervous breakdown at her first Yale interview and how she'd ended the session by kissing her interviewer. He'd also heard about her brief flirtation in a hotel room with her *alumni* interviewer. In a way, he was responsible for both mishaps. Whenever they broke up, Blair went completely apeshit.

He reached over and adjusted the ruby ring on her finger. "Relax. Everything's going to be okay," he told her soothingly. "I promise."

"Okay," Blair agreed, although the truth was she wasn't going to stop stressing until she had the Yale acceptance letter hanging above her bed in a custom-made silver Tiffany frame. She'd turn on the new Raves CD that always made her horny, even though it was kind of loud and obnoxious, and lie down on the bed, reading her acceptance letter over and over while Nate ravaged her naked body—

"Good." Nate leaned in and began to kiss her, interrupting her little X-rated fantasy.

Blair groaned inwardly. If only she could have sex with him right there on the greasy old wooden Central Park bench! But she had to wait until she heard from Yale. It was the deal she'd made with herself.

the only thing she hasn't got

At the other end of the promenade Serena van der Woodsen was eating a Fudgsicle and minding her own business when she spotted her two best friends on a park bench, devouring each other's faces and looking like an advertisement for true love. Serena sighed, walking slowly as she licked fudgey drips from the popsicle stick. If only true love was something you *could* buy.

Not that she hadn't had a gazillion boyfriends who were totally crazy in love with her and totally fun. There was Perce, the French boy who'd chased her in a little orange convertible all over Europe. Then there was Guy, the English lord who'd wanted to elope with her to Barbados. Conrad, the boy up at boarding school in New Hampshire, who'd kept her up till dawn, smoking cigars. Dan Humphrey, the morbid poet who never could find the right metaphor for her. Flow, the rock star turned stalker—not that she really *minded* being stalked by someone that hot and famous. And Nate Archibald, the boy she'd lost her virginity to and would love forever, but only as a friend.

And that was just the shortlist.

Still, she had never had that one *true* love, the kind of love Blair and Nate had.

She tossed the remains of her ice cream into a trash can and quickened her pace, her pink terrycloth Mella flip-flops slapping noisily on the paved walkway, her long, pale blond hair streaming out behind her, and her short gray pleated Constance Billard uniform flouncing against her endlessly long legs. As she drew near, the boys cavorting around Bethesda Fountain and skateboarding up and down the promenade pressed their inner pause buttons and turned to gape. Serena, Serena, Serena—she was everything they'd ever wanted.

Not that they'd ever have the guts to even say hi to her.

"Why don't you guys just get a room at the Mandarin? It's only a few blocks away," Serena joked when she reached her friends on the bench.

Nate and Blair looked up with happy, dazed expressions on their faces.

"Did you do the thing?" Serena asked Blair in that way only best friends can understand.

"Uh-huh," Blair nodded. "I didn't talk for very long, though, because Nate was totally listening."

"Was not!" Nate protested.

Serena glanced at Nate. "I just wanted to make sure Blair wasn't freaking out too much. I should have known you'd be able to calm her down."

Blair took a sip of lemonade. "Did you hear anything yet?"

Serena swiped the lemonade away from her. "No, for the fiftieth time today, I didn't hear anything yet." She took a drink and then wiped her mouth on the sleeve of her pale pink Tocca blouse. "Did you?"

Blair shook her head. Then she had an idea. "Hey, why don't we keep all our letters and then open them together? You know, so we can, like, freak out at the same time?"

Serena took another swig of lemonade. It sounded like the

worst idea she'd ever heard, but she was willing to risk getting her eyes clawed out to make her friend happy. "Okay," she agreed reluctantly.

Nate didn't say anything. No way did he want to join *that* little party. He held out his flask to Serena. "You want?"

She wrinkled her perfect nose and wiggled her unpolished toes. "Nah. I'm late for my pedicure. See you guys." Then she turned and walked south toward the end of the park, taking the half-empty can of lemonade with her.

She had a habit of picking things up without even realizing she was doing it. Lemonade, boys . . .

d rescues *v*, or the other way around

Vanessa waited patiently as Chuck Bass adjusted the red collar around the neck of his pet snow monkey so that the monogrammed *S* was visible to the camera. Chuck had wandered up to the fountain right after Blair left. He didn't even say hello, just sat down on the towel with his monkey and started talking.

"NYU better let me the fuck in, because I want to stay in the apartment my parents just bought me. And then me and Sweetie can stay together." Chuck ran his hands over the monkey's short white coat, his gold monogrammed pinky ring flashing in the sunlight. "I know he's only a monkey, but he's my best friend."

Vanessa zoomed in on the Prada logo on Chuck's black leather man-sandals. His toenails were freshly buffed, and a thin gold anklet hung loosely from his salon-tanned ankle. She'd been accepted early admission to NYU back in January. The idea that she and Chuck might be classmates next year was more than a little disturbing.

"'Course I'll rent a place wherever I go," Chuck continued. "But the decorator just did my apartment up in Armani Casa, and come on, who the fuck wants to live somewhere like Provi-fucking-dence, Rhode Island?"

★   ★   ★

Daniel Humphrey tossed the remains of his Camel cigarette into a pile of wet green leaves on the edge of the promenade. Zeke Freedman and a bunch of his other Riverside Prep classmates were playing roller hockey, and for a brief second he considered joining them. After all, Zeke used to be his best friend—before Dan hooked up with Vanessa Abrams, his other best friend. Now he was completely friendless, and that all seemed like a long time ago. He turned away, lit another Camel, and continued his ritual lonely after-school prowl across the park.

Bethesda Fountain on a sunny day wasn't really his scene—too many stoner jocks running around shirtless and tan girls listening to their iPods in Missoni bikinis—but it was a nice day, and he had nowhere else to be.

There were his little sister, Jenny, and her Constance Billard School friend Elise Wells, giving each other pedicures. There was that asshole Chuck Bass from his class at Riverside, sprawled at the base of the fountain with his monkey in his lap, talking to—

Dan ran a shaky hand through his overgrown boho-poet haircut and took a long drag on his cigarette. Vanessa hated the sun and hated guys like Chuck even more, but she'd put up with anything to make a good film. The willingness to suffer for their art was one of the many things she and Dan had in common.

He rifled through his messenger bag and pulled out a pen and the black leather-bound notebook he always carried, jotting down a few lines about the way Vanessa had worn the toes of her boots down until the metal showed through. Maybe it was the start of a new poem.

> *black*
> *steel-toed boots*

dead pigeons
dirty rain

"I'm making a documentary, if you want to be in it," Vanessa called over to him, cutting off Chuck in midsentence. Dan was wearing a cigarette-burned white undershirt and baggy tan cords. He looked like the same scruffy, disheveled poet she'd always known and loved. After his poem "Sluts" had been published in *The New Yorker,* Dan had started paying more attention to his look, buying clothes at French boutiques like Agnès B. and APC. It was right about then that he'd started cheating on Vanessa with that anorexic, yellow-toothed, poet-whore Mystery Craze. But Mystery was history, and maybe the old Dan was back for good.

The idea of sitting down and talking to Vanessa face-to-face was kind of unnerving, but perhaps if they just focused on the film, they wouldn't have to dig up all the ugly stuff. Dan glanced at Chuck, who was brushing his monkey with a child-sized pink tortoiseshell Mason Pearson hairbrush. "Are you—?"

"We're done." Vanessa dismissed Chuck. "Come back when you hear something."

Of course she didn't even have to say that. Chuck would be back. They all would. They couldn't help themselves. Getting self-absorbed people to dish their own dirt is so easy, it should be illegal.

"But I didn't get to the part about the publicist I hired for Sweetie," Chuck pouted. "We're going to get him on TV—"

"Save it," Vanessa barked. She tugged on the sleeve of her black button-down shirt and pretended to glance at her watch, when Dan knew for a fact she didn't even own one. "Next."

Chuck stood up and stalked away with his monkey on his

shoulder. Palms dripping with nervous sweat, Dan took his place. "So what's the film about?" he asked.

A girl lazing by the fountain dropped her lighter and Vanessa kicked it back with her boot. "I'm not sure yet. I mean, it has something to do with how crazy everyone is right now. You know, about college and everything," she explained. "But it's not just about *that*."

"Uh-huh." Dan nodded. Nothing Vanessa did was ever that simple. He dug around in his bag for his Camels and lit another one. "I have been kind of anxious about the mail lately," he admitted.

Vanessa peered into the camera and began to record. Dan's pale face looked so vulnerable in the sunlight, it was hard to believe he'd cheated on her—that he was capable of doing anything mean. "Go on."

"I think the thing that bugs me most is hearing the guys in my class say, 'Dude, I'm gonna miss you next year.'" Dan took a long drag on his cigarette. The apple-whiteness of Vanessa's inner arm made him forget what he was talking about. *Apple-white*, that was good.

"Go on," Vanessa prompted.

Dan blew smoke directly into the camera. "No one's going to miss me, and I'm not going to miss anyone, except for my dad and maybe my sister." He paused and swallowed hard. *And you and your apple-white arms*, he wanted to add, but decided he'd better write it down instead.

Vanessa tried to keep quiet, but Dan's little half-baked speech had moved her, even without the mention of her arms. "No one's going to miss me either," she declared, keeping her face pressed firmly against the viewfinder so they couldn't make eye contact.

Dan ashed on the ground and rubbed it in with the heel of

one of his scuffed blue Pumas. It felt weird to be talking to Vanessa in such a removed way when a little over a month ago they'd been in love and he'd had sex for the very first time. "*I'll* miss you," he admitted quietly. "I already miss you."

Why'd he have to be so goddamn cute?

Vanessa turned off the camera before she could say anything too revealing. "Camera's out of juice," she told him brusquely. "Maybe you could come back another day," she added, wishing she didn't always sound like such a bitch.

Dan pulled himself to his feet and hitched his messenger bag over his shoulder. "Good seeing you," he replied with a shy smile.

Unable to restrain herself, Vanessa smiled back. "You too." She hesitated. "Promise you'll come back when you hear any news?"

It was kind of nice to see her smile at him again. "I promise," Dan said earnestly, before loping back down the promenade.

Maybe she was only adjusting the lens, but it kind of looked like Vanessa was checking out his butt through the camera as he walked away.

oh, to be young and worry-free

"So nice of your brother, Daniel, to stop by," Elise Wells commented sarcastically to Jenny Humphrey. She stretched her long, freckled arms up over her head and then let them fall to her sides. "I think he's afraid of me."

Jenny removed her feet from Elise's lap and examined her freshly painted toes. Elise had smeared MAC New York Apple red polish all over her pinky toe, where the nail was supertiny, and it looked like she'd bludgeoned her foot with a hammer. "Dan's been acting like a freak lately," she noted. "And I hate to break it to you, but I don't think it has anything to do with you. He's supposed to hear back from colleges this week."

The two girls were seated on the opposite side of Bethesda Fountain from where Vanessa had set up her camera. Jenny shielded her eyes from the sun and peered over the fountain's rim to see what was going on.

Vanessa was filming Nicki Button now—another Constance Billard senior. It was common knowledge that Nicki had had two nose jobs. If you lined up her yearbook picture from the last three years, you could totally tell.

"She's only interviewing seniors," Elise stated. She tucked

her thick, strawlike blond bob behind her freckled ears. "I asked her at school during recess."

Jenny frowned. How come the seniors always got to do all the cool stuff? She pulled her bra down where it always rode up under her arms. Trickles of sweat had collected in the bra's cups, making it feel more like a wet suit than one of Bali's supersupportive comfort bras for big-breasted women. "It's not like I want to be in her stupid movie anyway," she muttered.

"Right," Elise scoffed. "Like you don't always try to copy everything Serena van der Woodsen does?"

Hello, meanness?

Jenny hugged her knees to her chest and glared at Elise defensively. Was she an internationally reknowned model? Was she blond? Did she wear a knee-length Burberry trench coat and smoke imported French cigarettes and walk around looking clueless while boys stared at her with her tongues wagging? Was she secretly the smartest girl in her class? No!

Actually, Jenny *was* the smartest girl in her class, but it was no secret.

"Name one thing I've done that Serena's done."

Elise unscrewed the little jar of nail polish that was resting on the fountain's edge and began painting her fingernails. The color looked garish and inappropriate against her pale, freckled skin. "It's not really what you've *done*. . . ." Her voice trailed off. "It's just how you're always so *buddy-buddy* with her during peer group. You know, like you want everyone to know you're friends with this *model*. And how you're always trying on all these fancy clothes in stores, like you'd really have anywhere to wear them, the way Serena does." She didn't even mention Jenny's brief dalliance with Nate Archibald, which had been such a blatant case of a freshman girl getting in over her head with an older guy, it was too embarrassing to bring up.

A soccer ball suddenly appeared out of nowhere and bounced off of Jenny's head. "Ow!" she exclaimed angrily, her face turning bright red. She stood up and shoved her feet into the pink suede DKNY mules she'd bought at the latest Bloomie's sale, messing up her still-wet toenails even more. "I don't know what your problem is," she snapped at Elise, "but I'd so much rather hang out with my freak of a brother than listen to you criticize me."

Infuriatingly enough, Elise kept on painting her fingernails.

"Fine," Jenny huffed, stomping down the steps and away from the fountain toward Central Park West. *Copy Serena,* she scoffed, her stupendous double-Ds bobbing with each step. *Like I could even come close.*

But Jenny wasn't one to take challenges lightly, and nothing would please her more than to prove to Elise that she wasn't just some wanna-be, hopelessly trying to copy Serena and failing every time. A boy whistled at her as she bobbed by, and she flipped her brown curly hair back from her face, pretending to ignore him. She might not be six feet tall and blond and gorgeous, but boys still whistled at her. That meant she had *something*, didn't it? And not all models were tall and blond. She lifted her chin and added a little strut to her walk, imitating the way the models walked in the runway shows she'd watched on the Metro Channel. Elise was going to eat her words when she saw Jenny's face on the pages of Vogue and Elle. She'd be such a success, even Serena would be jealous.

Although Serena wouldn't be too jealous of the pile of dog poop Jenny almost stepped in while trying to be the next Gisele.

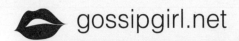

gossipgirl.net

Disclaimer: All the real names of places, people, and events have been altered or abbreviated to protect the innocent. Namely, me.

hey people!

The worst idea ever

So it's Thursday already and no one's heard anything yet. Hello?? And it's all due to this annoyingly dumb idea the U.S. Postal Service had. Apparently last year at this time, the postal service got millions of calls from college-bound seniors accusing them of losing their admissions letters and even tampering with the content of the letters. Right, like some mailman really cares if you got into Princeton or not. So this year they decided to try something called the National College Admission Letter Pool, which sounds a lot more intelligent than it really is. Basically it means that colleges are required to send their acceptance letters out in bundles according to zip code so the post office can deliver them all at once.

As if we haven't already suffered enough. Anyway, rumor has it the bundles went out on Monday, and since we all basically live in the same zip code, we should be getting ours, like . . . *TODAY!!*

Your e-mail

Dear GG,
You are the bomb. FYI, everyone: Party at my dad's restaurant tonight. True West, Pier Hotel, top floor, West Street. I've reserved a couple suites in the hotel too so there will be plenty of space to blow off steam. Stay cool.
—jay

A: Dear jay,
No, *you* are the bomb. See you tonight!
—GG

Sightings

B, harassing her mailman. It's because of people like her that we're all suffering right now! **S** reading the personal ads in *Time Out* during her **Mandarin Oriental Spa** pedicure. Interestingly enough, she was kind of stuck on the Women Seeking Women page. **D** sitting on the marble floor in the lobby of his apartment building right under the mailboxes, writing furiously in a little black notebook. Guess the pressure's getting to him. **N** drinking highballs with his parents at the **Yale Club**. Celebrating so early? **J** buying a three-foot-high stack of fashion magazines at her local newsstand. Is she researching a school assignment or just making a collage? And **V**, interviewing anybody and everybody. That's going to be one f'ed-up movie!

If you have a big dog who likes to bite mailmen, please keep him on a leash.

And remember people, *we're all in this together.*

You know you love me,

gossip girl

on your marks, get set, rrrip*!!*

"Oh my God, I can't breathe," Blair gasped dramatically. She hugged one of her stepbrother Aaron's barley-husk-filled bed pillows against her stomach. "I'm going to throw up."

It wouldn't be the first time.

"Calm down," Serena advised, arranging two little piles of white, cream, and manila envelopes on top of Aaron's eggplant-colored hemp bedspread. Her instincts in the park the other day about this little letter-opening party had been dead accurate. Blair was simply way too competitive to be civilized about the whole thing.

"I'm going to die," Blair moaned, clutching her stomach.

The two girls sat cross-legged on top of Aaron's bed in his bedroom, which was actually Blair's room from now until she went away to college. Her real bedroom was being made over into a nursery for Yale, her new baby half-sister, due to arrive in June. Aaron had moved in with her little brother, Tyler. Blair despised the room's ecofriendly décor and the persistent odor of stale soy hot dogs and herbal cigarettes. She was even thinking of petitioning for a suite at the Carlyle Hotel on Madison, at least until graduation.

Talk about a perfect setting for a post-getting-into-Yale rendezvous with Nate! But first things first: she had to get *in*.

On the bed between the two girls were two piles of envelopes, stacked facedown so that the return addresses were hidden. There were seven in Blair's stack and five in Serena's, yet Serena's stack was taller. There was no question about it: Serena's envelopes were suspiciously fatter.

"Okay. Ready?" Serena asked. She reached across the bed to give Blair's hand a little good-luck squeeze.

"Wait!" Blair grabbed the bottle of Ketel One vodka she'd swiped from her stepfather's nightstand and opened it with her teeth.

"The longer you drag it out, the more painful it's gonna be," Serena replied, beginning to lose patience.

Blair took a swig, then closed her eyes and reached for the first envelope in her stack. "Fuck it. Okay. Let's do it."

Rriipp!

Dear Ms. Waldorf,

The Office of Admissions is sorry to inform you that we have reviewed your application and cannot offer you a place at Harvard University next fall.

Rriipp!

Dear Ms. van der Woodsen,

The Office of Admissions has reviewed your application and is pleased to offer you a place at Harvard University. . . .

Rriipp!

Dear Ms. Waldorf,

Thank you for your application. Princeton University had an outstanding pool of applicants this year. The admissions decision is always a difficult one. We regret to inform you that we cannot offer you a place in the class of . . .

Rriipp!

Dear Ms. van der Woodsen,

Thank you for your outstanding application. Princeton University is pleased to offer you a place in the class of . . .

Rriipp!

Dear Ms. Waldorf,

We regret to inform you that Brown University cannot . . .

Rriipp!

Dear Ms. van der Woodsen,

The Office of Admissions was impressed with your application. We are pleased to invite you to join Brown University's class of . . .

Rriipp!

Dear Ms. Waldorf,

We have reviewed your application and have decided not to offer you a place at Wesleyan next fall. We wish you well.

Rriipp!

Dear Ms. van der Woodsen,

The Office of Admissions at Wesleyan University is pleased to offer you a place. . . .

Rriipp!

Dear Ms. Waldorf,

Vassar College is a small school and can only accept a limited number of applicants. We regret to inform you that we cannot offer you a place at Vassar next fall.

Rriipp!

Dear Ms. van der Woodsen,

Thank you for your application to Yale University. We are very pleased to invite you to join the class of . . .

Rriipp!

Dear Ms. Waldorf,

Thank you for your application to Yale University. The Office of Admissions has added your name to a wait list. The office will inform you of your status on or before June 15.

Rriipp!

Dear Ms. Waldorf,

    We have reviewed your application and are very pleased to offer you a place at Georgetown University next fall.

Blair tossed the last letter on top of the bedspread and seized the bottle of vodka. Wait-listed at Yale, and she only got into *Georgetown*? But that was her *safety*! No way had she thought she'd ever actually wind up there.

Drink up and think again, honey-pie.

She took a panicked gulp and then handed the bottle to Serena. "How'd you do?" she demanded.

Serena could tell from the scary look on Blair's face that the news was not good. She didn't know what to say. "Um, I got in . . . um . . . basically . . . everywhere?"

Blair stared disbelievingly at the sheaf of acceptance letters in Serena's hands. On top was a cream-colored letter marked with the distinctive blue Yale University letterhead. Her vision blurred. "Wait, you applied to Yale?"

Serena nodded. "At the last minute I just decided, why not, you know?"

"And you got *in*?"

Serena nodded again. "Sorry." She reached for the remote and flicked on Aaron's TV. Then she flicked it off again. The way Blair was glaring at her with her teeth bared was making her nervous.

Blair kept on glaring. Back in first grade she'd accidentally chopped off a foot-long swath of Serena's long golden hair with a steak knife. All these years she'd felt sort of guilty about it—until now. Now she wished she'd cut Serena's entire blond fucking head off. She snatched up the bottle and took another angry swig of vodka. What did *Serena* have that she didn't? She was in the top of her class at Constance and took every AP course they offered. She'd aced the SAT. She did charity work. She ran the French club. She was a ranked tennis player. Her entire high-school career—practically her whole life—she'd been working toward getting into Yale. Her father had gone there. *His* father had gone there. Her great-uncle had donated two buildings and a playing field. Serena had been kicked out of boarding school that fall. She took no APs at all, did hardly any extracurriculars, was purported to have mediocre grades and even lower SAT scores than Nate. Serena's dad had gone to Princeton and Brown, two of Yale's biggest competitors. Still, Yale had accepted Serena and stuck Blair on their fucking wait list! Was there something Serena knew that she didn't even after twelve two-hour sessions with Ms. Glos, the uptight, wig-wearing Constance Billard School senior guidance counselor, and one hundred and fourteen weeks of SAT prep??

"I probably won't even go," Serena faltered in an attempt to play things down. "I have to . . . you know . . . visit all the schools before I decide." She gathered her luxurious blond hair on top of her head and frowned. "Maybe I won't even go to college right away. I could stay in the city and try to do some acting or something."

Blair scooted off the bed, scattering her pile of rejection letters. So Serena got into Yale, but she didn't even really want to go there? "What the fuck?!" she cried, sloshing vodka all over the natural-sea-grass mat beneath her feet.

Serena collected her letters and held them behind her back. "What about the other schools? You must have—"

All of a sudden Blair's stepbrother, Aaron Rose, poked his smug, dreadlocked Rasta, into-Harvard-early-admission head into the room. "I thought I heard shouting." He squinted at the letters in Serena's hand. "Accepted at Harvard!" He walked into the room and held his hand up to give her a high five. "*Nice!*" He grinned over at Blair. "Wuzzabout you, sis?"

Blair wasn't sure whether to kill them both or kill herself. "I'm not your sister," she spat back. She slammed the half-empty vodka bottle down on the top of Aaron's organically grown–beechwood dresser, nearly breaking the glass bottle. "But since you're both obviously so interested, I got fucking *wait-listed* at Yale. The only place that accepted me is Georgetown. Fucking stupid-ass Georgetown."

Serena and Aaron stared at her for a moment, their eyes wide with a mixture of disbelief and fear of the Mighty Wrath of Blair.

"That's not so bad," Serena murmured finally. She didn't know much about Georgetown, but she'd met some cute boys who went there, and it might be kind of cool to live in the same city as the president. "I'm sure Yale is just playing hard to get. And if you don't wind up getting in, at least you have backup."

It was easy for Serena to talk about backup when her backup schools were Harvard and Brown. Blair stuffed her feet back into her new dove gray Eugenia Kim flats and snatched her black DKNY zip-up cardigan off the bed.

"Come on, Blair, don't be such sore loser. New Haven's a dump anyway. You'd probably hate it there." Aaron hooked his guitar-playing-callused thumbs into the pockets of his army green cargo pants. "At least they have a Prada in DC."

Of course the only thing Blair had heard him say was the word *loser*.

"Fuck off," she hissed to both of them as she stomped out

the door on her way over to Nate's house. Chances were Nate had only been accepted at some lame stoner school like Hobart or UNH. At least he could sympathize.

He'd probably even have sympathy sex. Not that she was even close to being in the mood.

n's news is too good to share

No one else was even home, but out of sheer habit, Nate stuffed a rolled-up navy blue Ralph Lauren bath towel into the space between the hardwood floor and his closed bedroom door before sitting down on his green-and-black-plaid bedspread and lighting up. He took a big hit and then reached for the first envelope in the short stack on his bedside table. He tore it open.

> Congratulations, Mr. Archibald,
>
> Brown University is pleased to offer you . . .

Score!

Nate dropped the letter on the bed, took another hit, and then tore open the second envelope.

> Dear Mr. Archibald,
>
> The Office of Admissions has reviewed your application and would like to invite you to join Boston University's class of . . .

Double score!

He sucked on the joint and then balanced it on the edge of his bedside table. Next envelope.

> Hampshire College had a strong and interesting pool of applicants this year. Yours stood out. Mr. Archibald, we are pleased to offer you a place at Hampshire next fall.

Triple score!

Last envelope—he'd only been able to deal with applying to four schools.

> Thank you for your application. Yale University's office of admissions is pleased to offer you a place in the class of . . .

Quadruple fucking score!!!

Nate couldn't wait to tell Blair. They could go to Yale together, live in the married people's housing just like she used to dream about. They could even get a dog, maybe. A Great Dane.

Nate examined the other paperwork stuffed inside the envelopes. Along with the acceptance letters from Brown and Yale were extra letters from the schools' lacrosse coaches, promising him a starting place on the team. "Holy shit," Nate breathed, reading the letters. They didn't just want him. They wanted him *bad*.

Join the club.

He reached for his cell phone and was about to speed-dial Blair's private line when the phone rang in his hand. The name BLAIR appeared on the phone's little screen.

"Hey. I was about to call you," Nate chuckled. "How'd it go?"

"Buzz me in." Blair replied in a clipped tone. "I'm like two doors away from your house."

Uh-oh.

Nate licked his fingers and pinched the burning end of the joint until it went out. Then he squirted a little Hermès Eau d'Orange Verte cologne into the air to freshen up the room. Not that he was trying to completely hide the fact that he'd been smoking weed; he just didn't want to gross Blair out with the smell.

The doorbell rang and he buzzed her in. "I'm in my room," he said into the high-tech video-intercom system.

"Come on up."

On the bed were his four acceptance letters. He gathered them up, eager to present Blair with the awesome news: they were both going to Yale! This particular strain of pot always made him horny. Maybe Blair would finally be ready to have sex, and they could celebrate properly, with their clothes *off*.

Or maybe not.

Nate's house was even nicer than Blair's—after all, it was a whole *house* with a garden and everything, and since he was an only child, Nate even had his own floor. But the stairs always annoyed Blair. Couldn't his parents just install an escalator?

"I'm dying," Blair wailed as soon as she reached the top step. She staggered into Nate's room and flopped facedown on the bed. Then she rolled over and stared up at the clear blue sky through the skylight in the ceiling. "At least, I wish I were dead."

The odds were pretty high that Blair wouldn't be considering death if she'd gotten into Yale. Nate slid his acceptance letters onto his desk and sat down next to her. Gingerly, he brushed his thumb against her flawlessly smooth cheek.

Thank you, La Mer skin cream.

"What's going on?" he asked gently.

"That stupid bitch Serena got into Yale and every other fucking school she applied to, and I only got into fucking Georgetown. Yale *wait-listed* me, and I got rejected everywhere else." Blair rolled over and pressed her face into Nate's leg. Today was the day she was supposed to have lost her virginity, but now it was obvious: she was too big a loser to *ever* have sex. "Oh, Nate. What are we going to do?"

Nate didn't know what to say. One thing was certain. He wasn't about to tell Blair that he'd gotten into Yale, too. She might smother him with a pillow or something. "I know a bunch of guys who got wait-listed at schools last year. Most of them wound up getting in," he offered.

"Yeah, but not to *Yale*," Blair moaned. "All the shitty schools have superlong wait lists because the kids using them as their safeties wind up not going."

"Oh."

Typical Blair. Her idea of a shitty school was any school other than Yale.

"Yale knows that almost everyone they accept is going to go, so their wait list probably has, like, two people on it, and those two people are totally *never* going to get in." She sighed dramatically. "Fuck!" Then she sat up and flicked a piece of lint off her Seven jeans. "So what about you? Where'd you get in?"

Nate knew it was wrong to withhold information from his girlfriend—the girl he loved—but he couldn't bear to break her heart.

Or make her so mad she wouldn't want to fool around?

"Um," he yawned, like this was the most boring conversation ever. "Hampshire. BU. Brown. That's about it."

So he forgot to mention Yale. That wasn't the same as lying, was it?

Um, yes?

Blair stared icily at the bare hardwood floor, twirling her ruby ring around and around on her finger so fast it made Nate dizzy. He lay down next to her and wrapped his arms around her waist. "Georgetown is a good school."

Blair's body was rigid. "But it's so far away from Brown," she complained.

Nate shrugged and began to massage the spot between her shoulder blades. "Maybe I'll go to BU. I bet there's a shuttle from Boston to DC."

Tears welled in Blair's eyes and she kicked at the mattress with her heels. "But I don't want to go to Georgetown. I *hate* Georgetown!"

Nate pulled her head to his chest and kissed her neck. He and Blair hadn't been on his bed together like this in months, and he was getting seriously horny. "Have you even been down there to check it out?"

As a matter of fact, Blair hadn't visited any school other than Yale. "No," she admitted.

Nate ran his tongue over her earlobe. The peachy smell of her shampoo was giving him the munchies. "I've met a lot of cool girls from Georgetown. You should go down there. Maybe you'll even like it better than Yale," he said, his voice muffled as he nuzzled her neck.

"Right," Blair responded bitterly. She was vaguely aware that Nate was coming on to her, but she was so upset, all she could feel was his spit on her ear. Nate fell back on the bed and pulled her on top of him. His eyes were closed and his lips were pressed together in a stoned, happy, turned-on smile.

"Mmm," he moaned, enjoying the weight of her on top of him.

"I just wish I'd gotten into Yale," Blair whispered. Then she could whip off her clothes and they could finally do it, just as she'd always imagined. She tucked her head into the crook of Nate's chin and breathed in his nice smoky scent. All she needed right now was a good cuddle. Sex would just have to wait.

Nate opened his eyes and sighed heavily. *Coitus Interruptus, Part XX,* produced especially for him by Blair Waldorf.

Not that he actually *deserved* sex.

"Just promise me you'll check out Georgetown," he said, trying to sound like a good supportive boyfriend and not a lying son of a bitch.

Blair hugged him tight. Her life was a miserable pit of hell, and her best friend was a deceitful bitch, but at least she had Nate—adorable, caring, straightforward Nate. And he was right. Visiting Georgetown couldn't hurt. At this point she'd do anything.

"Okay. I promise," she agreed.

Nate tucked his hand inside the waistband of her jeans but she grabbed it and pulled it out again.

Well, *almost* anything.

and the winner is . . .

"He's here!" Dan heard his kid sister, Jenny, whisper as he closed the front door of the apartment. "Hurry!"

He dropped his keys on the rickety old table in the front hall and kicked off his Pumas. "Hello?" he called, padding into the kitchen, where the family usually converged. As usual, Marx, the Humphreys' enormous black cat, lay sprawled on the cracked yellow Formica kitchen table, his head resting on an orange dish towel. Dan's half-empty coffee cup was right where he'd left it that morning, near Marx's little pink nose. The kitchen lights were on, and a half-eaten Dannon fat-free blueberry yogurt—Jenny's favorite—sat on the yellow countertop. Dan tugged on Marx's furry black ears. The usual pile of mail was suspiciously missing from the table, and Jenny was nowhere in sight. "Yo. Anyone home?" he called.

"In here," Jenny's voice rang out from the adjacent dining room.

Dan pushed open the swinging door to the dining room. Side by side at the scratched Pennsylvania Dutch farm table sat Jenny and their dad, Rufus. Rufus was wearing a heather gray Mets T-shirt, and his wild and wiry gray beard was badly in need of combing. Jenny was wearing an expensive-looking silk tiger-print halter top, and her nails were painted bright red. In the empty place across from them sat a stack of envelopes, an unopened box of Entenmann's chocolate donuts, and a white paper cup of deli coffee.

"Have a seat, son. We've been waiting for you," Rufus explained with an anxious smile. "We even got your favorite donuts. Today's the big day!"

Dan blinked. For the past seventeen years his father had complained about the cost of raising and educating two ungrateful teenagers, and constantly threatened to move to a country where medicine and education were publicly funded. Yet he sent Dan and Jenny to two of the most expensive and competitive single-sex private schools in Manhattan, taped their stellar report cards to the fridge, and was constantly quizzing them on poetry and Latin. He seemed even more freaked out about Dan's college acceptance letters than Dan was.

"Did you guys already open my mail?" Dan demanded.

"No. But we will if you don't hurry up and sit down," Jenny told him. She tapped the stack of envelopes with a shiny red fingernail. "I put Brown on top."

"Gee, thanks," Dan grumbled as he sat down. As if the whole process wasn't nerve-racking enough. He hadn't anticipated opening his mail in front of an audience.

Rufus reached across the table for the box of donuts and tore it open. "Go on," he urged, before stuffing a donut into his mouth.

His fingers trembling, Dan carefully opened the envelope from Brown and unfolded the sheets of paper inside.

"Oh my God, you're so in!" Jenny squealed.

"What'd they say? What'd they say?" Rufus demanded, his bushy gray eyebrows twitching excitedly.

"I got in," Dan told them quietly. He handed his father the letter.

"Of course you did!" Rufus gloated. He grabbed last night's nearly empty bottle of Chianti from off the table, uncorked it with his teeth, and took a swig. "Go on, open the next one!"

The second letter was from New York University—NYU—where Vanessa had been accepted early admission.

"I bet you're in," Jenny anticipated annoyingly.

"Shhhh!" her father hissed at her.

Dan tore open the letter. He looked up at their expectant faces and announced evenly, "In."

"Whoo-hoo!" Rufus cheered, slapping his chest like a proud gorilla. "Atta boy!"

Jenny reached for the next envelope. "Can I open this one?"

Dan rolled his eyes. Did he have any choice? "Sure."

"Colby College," Jenny read. "Where's that?"

"Maine, you ignoramus," their father answered. "Will you open it please?"

Jenny giggled and slid her finger under the flap of the envelope. This was fun, like being a presenter at the Oscars or something. "And the Oscar goes to . . . Dan! You're in!"

"Cool." Dan shrugged. He hadn't even gone up to Maine to visit Colby, but his English teacher insisted it had the best writing program on the East Coast.

Jenny reached for the next envelope and tore it open without even asking for permission first. "Columbia University. Oops. They rejected you."

"Bastards," Rufus growled.

Dan shrugged again. Columbia had a prestigious and demanding creative writing program, and it was so close to home he wouldn't have needed to live in a dorm. But considering the claustrophobic situation he found himself in right now, living at home for the next four years seemed kind of unappealing.

The last envelope was from Evergreen College in Washington State, so far away it had a sort of romantic appeal. He slid the envelope across the table to Rufus and picked up his complimentary cup of coffee. "Open it, Dad."

"Evergreen!" Rufus bellowed. "Abandoning us for the Pacific Northwest! Do you have any idea how much it rains out there?"

"Dad," Jenny whined.

"All right, all right." Rufus tore open the envelope, ripping the letter in the process. He squinted at the mangled sheet of paper. "In!" He grabbed another donut, shoved it in his mouth, and then pushed the box toward Dan. "Four out of five—not too shabby!"

"Let's eat out to celebrate!" Jenny cried, clapping her hands. "There's this new restaurant on Orchard Street that is supposed to be really cool. All the models go there."

Rufus grimaced at Dan. "Before you arrived, your sister announced that she is going to be a supermodel. Apparently by the end of the month I'll be riding around in my jet buying racehorses and boats with all the millions she's going to make." He pointed a chocolatey finger at Jenny. "You'll cover Dan's college tuition, too, right?"

Jenny rolled her eyes. "Dad."

Rufus squinted at her. "Where'd you get that shirt, anyway?" His forehead grew red and shiny, the way it did when he was excited. "If you don't stop misusing my credit card, I'm sending you to boarding school. You hear?"

Jenny rolled her eyes again. "You may not have to send me. I'll be happy to go."

Dan cleared his throat noisily and stood up. "That's

enough, kids. There's a party later on tonight, but before I go, you can take me out for Chinese. At my place on Columbus."

"Bor-ing," Jenny moaned.

"You got it," Rufus agreed, winking at him. "By the way, I vote for NYU. That way you can live at home, I can help you study, and in return you can hook me up with some of your brainy female English professors."

Dan felt like he'd stepped into a corny Disney movie about horny stay-at-home dads. He grabbed a donut out of the box, scooped up the pile of letters, and headed into his room. A blank notebook lay on the unmade bed, waiting for him to pick it up and fill it with somber, tortured verse. But Dan was too happy to write. He'd gotten into four out of the five schools he'd applied to! He couldn't wait to share the good news.

The problem was, with whom?

as long as he's happy, she's happy

"What if he's home all alone slashing his wrists or something?" Vanessa fretted out loud. She glared at her twenty-two-year-old sister Ruby's leather-clad ass. Ruby was leaning in her bedroom doorway, talking on the landline and her cell phone at the same time, organizing her band's upcoming tour.

"Iceland!" Ruby shouted. "We're number five on the indie charts in freaking Reykjavík!"

"Big freaking whoop," Vanessa growled, checking her e-mail for the sixtieth time, even though no one ever e-mailed her. She had convinced herself that Dan had been rejected from every school he'd applied to and was at that very moment standing on top of the George Washington Bridge, writing his postscript before he jumped. Even if he had gotten in somewhere, he was probably having some sort of existential apocalyptic moment and was right now wading naked into the Hudson River near the boat basin to cleanse himself of all the creativity-draining negative karma before he could write again.

If she were being honest with herself, she'd admit that she wasn't really all that worried. Dan was a good student and a brilliant writer. He was bound to get in somewhere. All she really wanted was an excuse to call him up and talk to him again, because ever since she'd seen Dan in the park on Monday, she couldn't stop thinking about him.

She'd thought about calling him under the pretense of another interview for her documentary, but that was so obvious, just thinking about it made her break out into a rash. She'd also thought of calling Dan's little sister, Jenny, under the pretense of asking her to do an interview on what it was like to have a sibling in the throes of getting into college. Then Jenny would blurt to Dan that Vanessa had called and asked about him, and then maybe Dan would call or e-mail *her*. But come on, how sixth grade could you get?

Ruby was still parked in her doorway, talking on the phone. This was the problem with Ruby sleeping in the living room and Vanessa having the only bedroom: Ruby treated Vanessa's bedroom like *her* living room.

"Hold on. Call-waiting," Ruby told the person on the other end of the line. She plugged her nose and put on a fake operator's voice. "All systems are busy at this time—" She paused. "Oh, hello, Daniel. Would you mind calling back? I'm on an important call with my band. We're taking over the universe."

Vanessa lunged for the phone and wrenched it out of Ruby's hand. "Hello?" she said tremulously. "Dan? Are you . . . are you okay?"

"Yup," Dan replied, sounding happier than she'd ever heard him sound. "I got in everywhere except Columbia."

"Wow!" Vanessa responded, absorbing the information. "But you want to go to Brown, right? I mean, you're not even really considering NYU or those other schools?"

"I don't know," Dan answered. "I have to think it over."

They were both silent for a moment. They'd discussed the

obvious, but there was so much more to discuss, it was kind of overwhelming.

"Well, anyway, congratulations," Vanessa managed to utter, suddenly feeling incredibly sad. Dan was going to Brown in Providence, Rhode Island, where he'd probably meet some long-haired, skinny girl from Vermont who made pottery and played guitar and knitted him sweaters, while she stayed in New York and went to NYU and continued to live with her freak of a sister.

Ruby grabbed the phone out of her hand. "Hey Dan, guess what? I'm going on tour for like eight months with SugarDaddy. We're leaving next week. Why don't you move in here? You and my sister can have, like, your own little love pad!"

Vanessa glared at her. Leave it to Ruby to completely mess things up in the most tactless, embarrassing way possible. Ruby handed back the phone and Vanessa held it a few inches away from her ear. *What the fuck was she supposed to say now?*

Dan wasn't opposed to the idea of living parent-free in a cool neighborhood like Williamsburg, and living with Vanessa might actually be kind of great. She could make her films, he could write. It would be like Yaddo—one of those retreats for writers and artists that his dad had gone to back in the old days. Maybe they'd even wind up getting back together and having lots of sex all the time, just like all those artists and writers were rumored to have done back in the seventies.

Still, everything was happening kind of fast. His cleared his throat. "I'll have to talk to my dad about it. We're going out for Chinese tonight to celebrate. How 'bout we meet at that party on West Street afterwards?"

Vanessa was hardly the partying type, but she supposed Dan had a reason to want to celebrate. "Sounds good," she agreed.

"And I'll talk to my dad about the moving-in thing. I think it could be kind of cool," Dan told her, sounding rather cool himself.

Vanessa suddenly felt like the girl in those cheesy happy-ending movies she'd always hated. The one who lives happily ever after with her adoring husband in a house with silk curtains in the windows instead of black sheets like she and Ruby had.

"*Cool*," she enthused, even though it had always been one of her least favorite words. She clicked off and handed the phone back to her sister, who was still jabbering on her cell phone. "Can I borrow some stuff from your closet?" Vanessa whispered.

Ruby cocked an eyebrow at her and nodded silently.

Looks like this is going to be some party.

like she was actually in the mood to celebrate?

Blair stepped off the elevator and stood staring at the home-made banner taped to the front door of the penthouse. "YAY, BLAIR! WE'RE SO PROUD OF YOU!" it read. She pushed open the door. Mookie, Aaron's exuberant brown-and-white boxer, waggled over and shoved his wet nose between her legs.

"Fuck off," Blair growled. For a brief moment she wondered if a miracle had occurred. Maybe her France-living gay dad or some other benevolent fairy had put in a call to Yale and they'd decided to accept her right away. It was unlikely, but—

"Serena told us what happened!" her pregnant mother crowed, swaying hugely in the foyer. "Wait list, shmait list. I can't imagine why you got so upset, darling. Yale has just as good as accepted you!"

Blair peeled off her cardigan and threw it on the antique chaise in the corner. Mookie threatened to sniff her crotch again and she kicked him away. "It's not that simple, Mom."

Pregnancy had made Eleanor's highlighted blond hair grow superfast, and it hung down to her shoulders in what Blair thought was a pathetic attempt to look like she was of appropriate childbearing age. Eleanor clapped her bejeweled hands together. "Well, my little sourpuss, we're having a special family celebration for you anyway. Everyone's waiting in the dining room!"

A family celebration. Oh, goody.

The table was laid with Eleanor's finest crystal and silver, and she'd ordered in from Blue Ribbon Sushi, Blair's favorite. Cyrus and Aaron were already merry with champagne. Even twelve-year-old Tyler looked a little drunk.

"And you thought you'd wind up at Norwalk Community College," Aaron said as he poured champagne into Blair's empty glass. "We all knew you could do better."

Cyrus winked at her with one of his bulbous, bloodshot, muddy blue fish eyes. "Yale rejected me flat when I applied. It's about time I made them sorry. If you'd like me to give them a kick in the pants about your application, I'd sure enjoy doing it."

Blair grimaced. As if she wanted Yale to know she and Cyrus were even remotely related?!

"I'm not going to college," Tyler announced, sipping his champagne like a pro. "I'm going to DJ in clubs all over Europe. And then I'm going to open a casino."

"We'll see about that." Eleanor forked a six-inch-long California roll onto her plate and giggled. "Baby's hungry again."

Blair had a feeling her mother wouldn't look like she was twenty months pregnant instead of only seven if she'd stop eating so much. She downed her entire glass of champagne and reached for an untouched box of sushi. First she was going to stuff her face with eel roll and pour enough champagne down her throat to make her puke her guts out. Then she was going to meet Nate at that stupid party on West Street, but only for ten minutes, because watching everyone celebrate when she had nothing to celebrate was going to make her puke even more. And then she was going to fall asleep watching *Breakfast at Tiffany's,* her all-time-favorite movie, starring her all-time-favorite star. Audrey Hepburn hadn't even gone to college, but she'd still had a charmed life.

Her mother picked up her log of sushi and bit into it like a hot dog. She and Cyrus had known each other for less than a year and had only been married since November, but Eleanor seemed to have picked up his eating habits. She put the remaining sushi down and dabbed her lips with a white linen napkin.

"Now that we're all gathered here, I have a favor to ask you, darling."

Blair looked up from her eel. It appeared her mother was addressing her.

Oh, boy.

"You know it's been a while, so my doctor thought it might be good for me to take a childbirth class, to refresh my memory. I signed up for the intensive one. It meets four afternoons for two hours. The thing is, Cyrus is working on his new project out in the Hamptons, and he's rather squeamish about these kinds of things anyway. Do you think you could come with me, darling? I have to have a partner, and it's only a couple of hours after school."

Blair coughed the rest of the eel into her napkin and lunged for her champagne. *Childbirth class?* What the fuck? "I thought Aaron was the one who wanted to be a doctor," she complained. "Why can't he go?"

"You always take such good care of your mother," Cyrus told her.

"I have band practice," Aaron said. As if he'd ever planned on volunteering.

"Me too," Tyler put in quickly.

And it wasn't as though Eleanor could ask any of her middle-aged socialite friends to go with her. Their children were all college-age, or nearly. To them, Eleanor's pregnancy was a tremendous, horrifying embarrassment.

"Fine. I'll go," Blair agreed sullenly. She pushed her plate away and stood up. The thought of talking to them any longer made her want to puke already. Besides, everyone seemed to have forgotten what they were supposed to be celebrating, anyway. "May I be excused?" she asked. "I have to get ready to go out."

Her mother reached over and snaked an arm around her. "Of course, darling." She gave Blair's waist a squeeze. "You're my best friend."

Ew?

Blair wriggled free and escaped to her so-called bedroom. At least Georgetown was further away than Yale—it had that going for it. And it wouldn't hurt to call the number on the acceptance letter and make arrangements for a visit.

If only she'd applied to the University of Australia.

She peeled off her jeans and T-shirt and made a half-hearted effort to dress for the party, putting on a tighter, darker pair of jeans and a black sleeveless shirt. Her arms looked pale and slack, and she pinched them angrily.

"Hey sis," Aaron called from outside her door. "Can I come in?"

Blair rolled her eyes at her reflection in her bedroom mirror. "It's not like I can stop you," she replied miserably.

Aaron opened the door, wearing his Harvard T-shirt like the asshole he was. It was kind of a tradition to wear an article of clothing from the school you wanted to go to right after finding out that you'd gotten in, but Aaron had found out months ago. "I thought we could head down to the party together."

"Fine," Blair sighed. "I'm almost ready." She picked up a stick of Chanel eyeliner and drew a dark gray line beneath each of her eyes. Then she smeared on some MAC Ice lip gloss and ran her fingers through her hair. There. Done.

"Aren't you going to wear your Yale T-shirt?" Aaron asked, watching as she searched under the bed for an appropriate pair of shoes. "I won't tell anyone about the wait list."

"Gee, thanks," Blair retorted as she shoved her feet into a pair of boring black Coach loafers. She yanked the bedroom door open all the way and stomped down the hall, not even caring that her tight jeans made her bulky cotton underwear bunch and ride right up her butt.

So much for the days of dressing for success!

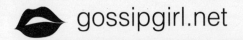

gossipgirl.net

Disclaimer: All the real names of places, people, and events have been altered or abbreviated to protect the innocent. Namely, me.

hey people!

How to get off the wait list and into the college of your choice

Stage a hunger strike in front of the admissions office.

Take the SATs *again*, cheat, and get a perfect score.

Learn to play "Yankee Doodle" on the violin and serenade the admissions office until they beg you to enroll, if only you'll stop playing.

Buy more shoes than Imelda Marcos, get in the *Guinness Book of World Records*, write a tell-all memoir, and win the Pulitzer Prize for literature.

Use your platinum Amex to buy the dean of admissions that new BMW convertible all your guy friends want for graduation.

Your e-mail

 Dear GG,
I met this boy a while ago at a party in NYC. He totally convinced me he was going to Georgetown next year and would be captain of our lax team. He was going to keep his sailboat somewhere nearby and we were going to sail down to Florida together for spring break. I never heard from him again, and now I don't think he even applied.
—brokenhrt

 Dear brokenhrt,
Guess he must have found another port to dock his ship in. I'm so sorry.
—GG

Q: Dear GG,

I heard that dumb blond Constance girl got in everywhere because she slept with all her interviewers.

—beast

A: Dear beast,

I don't know if we're even talking about the same blond Constance girl. But maybe she's a lot smarter than everyone thinks.

—GG

Q: Dear GG,

Just so you and everyone else knows, I work in the admissions office at the Dorna B. Rae College for Women in Bryn Mawr, Pennsylvania, and we are still accepting applications. Come and check us out!

—camil

A: Dear camil,

Sounds tempting. I'll def. make sure **B** knows about this, and anyone else who's really desperate.

—GG

Sightings

N and his buds celebrating their acceptances on the roof terrace of his town house. Passersby were getting high on the secondhand smoke. That old girlfriend of **N**'s from **Greenwich**—you remember, the crazy, drug-addicted heiress?—at a convent in **Sweden**, "reforming." **J** having a free makeup consultation at the **Clinique** counter in **Bloomingdale's SoHo**. It's important to know your pore size and what type of exfoliator to use before you become a famous supermodel. **V**, also in Bloomingdale's SoHo, getting made over by a glamorous transvestite at the **MAC** counter. Hot date tonight? **S** at an ATM withdrawing a hot-pink alligator **Birkin** bag full of cash. Paying off the admissions offices at all the schools she got into? Making a contribution to charity? Buying herself an "I got in!" gift at one of those exclusive **meatpacking district** boutiques that only take cash? **D** with his dad in a Broadway liquor store, buying a magnum of Dom. That's one proud papa. And **B** returning a get-lucky outfit in **Barneys'** lingerie department. Guess she decided it was bad luck.

I believe I have a little college acceptance celebrating to do myself.

See you at the party tonight!

You know you love me,

gossip girl

n has something to confess

True West was one of those places that felt brand-new every night, but it was also so classic, it might have been around forever. The walls were covered in mirrors with the drinks menus and specials scrawled all over them in waxy orange crayon. White leather horseshoe-shaped banquettes were scattered haphazardly around the dining room, and on each table a faux deerskin served as a tablecloth. Waiters dressed in denim Dries van Noten tunics and turquoise snakeskin cowboy boots wielded cocktails on vintage orange cafeteria trays. Weird Japanese country music drifted through the air, and behind the bar stood a wall of orange-tinted windows looking out over the Hudson River.

Except for her battered black combat boots, Vanessa was barely recognizable in a black stretch faux-leather miniskirt and fluttery red-and-black zebra-print shirt. Thanks to the nice transvestite at the Bloomingdale's SoHo MAC counter, her lips were painted red, and her eyebrows had been plucked for the first time ever. She stationed herself on a stool at the far end of the bar and propped her camera upon her shoulder.

The party had a giddy, first-day-of-school vibe. Girls in matching BU T-shirts squealed and threw their arms around one another. Boys in Brown sweatshirts gave each other high fives. Vanessa observed them silently, waiting for one of them to approach her and volunteer for an interview.

"I think I have something to say," announced an extraordinarily handsome boy wearing khakis and a plain white button-down shirt. He set his Tanqueray gin and tonic on the bar and took a seat on the stool next to Vanessa. "Do you want me to tell you my name and what school I go to and all that?" he asked.

Vanessa trained the camera on his bloodshot but still glittering green eyes. "Not unless you want to," she replied. "Just tell me a little bit about how the getting-in process has been for you."

Nate took a sip of his drink and looked out the orange-tinted windows. Across the river, planes circled over Newark Airport.

"The funny thing is, I wasn't really stressed out until now," he admitted. He pulled a Marlboro Light out of a pack someone had left behind and rolled it back and forth on top of the bar. "And the stupid thing is, I shouldn't be stressed out. I should be celebrating."

He glanced at the camera and then looked away self-consciously. Behind him the banquettes were filling up, and suddenly the music was so loud, he could barely hear himself think. "I don't know why I didn't tell her I applied," he mumbled.

"Who?" Vanessa coaxed. "Where?

"My girlfriend," Nate explained. "See, she really wants to go to Yale. Like, it's the most important thing in her life. I wound up applying there because they have a new lacrosse coach who brought them up from a shitty division-two team to the leading division-one team in less than a year. Anyway, today I found out that I got in and she only got wait-listed. I never even told her I applied, and I guess I'm kind of scared to tell her I got in. I mean, we only just got back together. And if I tell her, she'll break up with me again."

He waited for Vanessa to respond. When she didn't, he reached for his drink.

"The coaches from Yale and Brown are coming down this weekend to watch me play. Blair's going down to DC to look at Georgetown, so luckily I won't have to lie to her about where the coaches are from and all that." Nate splayed his elbows and let his chin fall into his hands.

Kind of sucks to be a liar, doesn't it?

All of a sudden the familiar scent of a certain patchouli essential-oil mixture filled his nostrils.

"We did it, Natie!" Serena breathed as she threw her arms around Nate's neck. Her pale blond hair was piled into a messy knot on top of her head and she was wearing a filmy white-and-gold-fringed poncho shirt over white jeans.

Very Las Vegas showgirl meets *The OC*.

Nate kissed her cheek and tried to look as psyched as he should have.

"Oops." Serena grimaced, immediately catching on. "Did Blair break up with you again?"

"Not yet." Nate was about to explain the whole thing, but then Blair stepped off the elevator at the opposite end of the enormous restaurant, glaring angrily at Serena's back as she approached.

At one of the banquettes, a group of Constance Billard seniors began to whisper among themselves.

"I heard Blair wrote this really dumb screenplay instead of an essay for her Yale application. Ms. Glos told her to change it, but she sent it anyway, and that's why she didn't get in,"

Nicki Button told her friend Rain Hoffstetter. Rain and Nicki were going to Vassar together next year, and they couldn't stop looking at each other and squealing.

"I heard Blair wrote Serena's Yale essay for her. That's why she's so pissed off. She got Serena in, but she only got wait-listed," Isabel Coates told her best friend, Kati Farkas. Kati and Isabel had both gotten into Georgetown and Rollins, but Isabel had gotten into Princeton and she was already wearing her Princeton T-shirt. The idea of splitting up was so heart-breaking, they couldn't stop holding hands.

"Well I heard Serena got a 1560 on her SAT. She pretends to be so flaky and dumb, but it's all a big act. That's how she can go out so much and never study. She doesn't have to," Kati stated jealously.

"What are you guys talking about?" Blair demanded when she reached the spot where Serena and Nate were seated at the bar. She'd only just arrived, but she hated the party already. She hated how many kids were wearing their stupid college T-shirts, she hated the queer Japanese country music blaring out of the stupid orange Bose speakers hanging over the bar, and she hated that Serena was talking to Nate in that intimate hands-all-over-over-him way she used whenever she talked to guys.

"Nothing!" Serena and Nate answered in unison.

Serena spun around on her bar stool. "Are you still mad at me?"

Blair crossed her arms over her chest. "How come you're not wearing a Yale T-shirt? Oh, that's right. You got in, but you're probably not going," she added sarcastically.

Serena shrugged. "I don't know. I'm visiting a bunch of places this weekend. Hopefully that will help me decide."

Nate's armpits grew suddenly damp. He slid off his bar

stool, put his hands on Blair's shoulders, and kissed her on the forehead. "You look pretty," he said in an effort to distract her from the subject of Yale.

"Thanks," Blair said even though she knew for a fact that she looked like a preppy, uptight bitch who never had any fun. She wasn't even wearing any earrings, for Christ's sake! Farther down the bar a group of girls in matching hunter green Dartmouth T-shirts shouted out some stupid Dartmouth song before doing a line of vodka shots.

"Ten minutes and then I'm leaving," Blair told Nate bluntly. "It's a school night, anyway."

As if that had ever kept her from partying before.

Nate kissed her temple. He was anxious to get her away from Serena before Serena innocently blurted out the news that he'd gotten into Yale, too. "Want to go check out the sunset or something?" he suggested lamely.

"Whatever," Blair replied, keeping her arms stubbornly crossed over her chest.

"Never mind me." Serena swung her bar stool around until she was facing Vanessa. "Okay, babe, I'm ready for my close-up."

Vanessa didn't need to adjust a thing. She'd been filming the whole time.

she's lost that lovin' feelin'

"So I guess I should be happy," Serena declared.

Vanessa tracked the camera slowly across Serena's flawless face and then panned down, looking for some physical defect or odd personality quirk to zoom in on. She couldn't find one. Then Serena stuck her thumbnail in her mouth and began to gnaw on it.

Aha!

She pulled her thumb away and frowned. "I *am* happy," she insisted, as though trying to convince herself. "I got into every school I applied to. They didn't even care about me not getting asked back to boarding school this year. It's just . . ." Her voice trailed off when she saw a boy and a girl, both dressed in Middlebury T-shirts, making out near the elevators. She sighed. "I just wish I had someone to celebrate with."

The music suddenly shifted from Japanese country to the quirky beats of the new Raves album. Two guys in U Penn baseball caps and yellow neckties peeled off their shirts, turned their hats around backwards, and began to break-dance. Then four drunk girls wielding Vanderbilt pennants took off *their* shirts and started trying to break-dance, badly.

"I used to dance on tables," Serena confessed, sounding

like some wistful, washed-up, middle-aged cabaret singer. "Now look at me."

Of course about ninety-nine percent of the room's male constituency *was* looking at her while they tried to come up with a pickup line good enough to get her to dance with them. In addition to the boys, a short, curly-haired, large-chested freshman girl was sizing Serena up as she considered how to approach her.

Jenny and Dan had only just arrived, leaving their emotional father waxing nostalgic in the family's favorite Upper West Side Chinese restaurant over a carafe of sweet white wine. They stood in front of the elevator doors, surveying the room.

"I warned you it would be obnoxious," Dan told his little sister. Normally Dan hated parties, and this particular scene should have annoyed the hell out of him, but he was feeling completely pleased with himself, and the party was the perfect setting for his mood.

But Jenny only had eyes for Serena. "Don't worry, I can handle it," she replied. Hiking up her tiger-print halter top, she pushed her way across the crowded room, making a beeline for the bar.

"If I deferred," Serena rambled on, "I could do some more modeling. And maybe some acting, too."

Jenny leaned against the bar as she waited for a chance to ask Serena for advice on how to break into modeling. Her whole body shook with anticipation, and she felt silly for being so nervous.

Dan only followed Jenny because he was worried she would order some sort of poisonous mixed drink and would need to be taken home before Vanessa even arrived. Then he noticed that Vanessa was already very much there, her camera propped up on her shoulder as she interviewed Serena for her film.

Her lips were painted dark red, a silver snake was clipped to her ear, and a slinky black skirt clung to her thighs. Her red-and-black tank top was sort of slipping over her bare shoulders, exposing her apple-white skin in a way Dan had never seen it exposed before. At least, not in public.

Without even pausing to think, he pushed his way through the dancing throng, walked up behind Vanessa, and kissed her neck. Her pale cheeks flushed pink and she whirled around on her bar stool, nearly dropping her beloved camera in the process.

"It's not like I have to go to college now—" Serena stopped in midsentence, staring as Vanessa and Dan groped each other like horny, sex-starved beasts.

Cut!

Jenny decided to make her move. She bumped her shoulder up against Serena's hip, hoping to give the appearance of running into her by accident. "Hey. So, congratulations and everything," she blurted out awkwardly. "That's a really cool shirt."

If Serena had been Blair or some other senior girl, she might have brushed Jenny off with a terse "Thank you" while wondering what this annoying freshman brat was even doing at a senior post-getting-into-college party. But Serena never brushed anyone off. It was one of the things that made her so irresistible, or so intimidating, depending on who you were and how badly you wanted her. Besides, Jenny just happened to be in the ninth-grade peer group Serena co-led with Blair, so it wasn't as if they were total strangers.

Jenny had a new haircut, with thick straight bangs and a curly bob that fell just to her chin. Her hair was dark and her brown eyes were big and round. The severe cut suited her.

"I love your hair!" Serena slid off her bar stool so Jenny wouldn't be the only one standing. "You look like that model in all the new Prada ads."

Jenny's big brown eyes almost popped out of her head. "Really? Thanks," she gasped, feeling like she'd been tapped on the shoulder with a magic wand.

The bartender came over and Serena ordered two glasses of champagne. "You don't mind drinking with me, do you?" she asked Jenny.

Jenny was flabbergasted. *Mind?* It was an absolute honor. She ran her finger over the damp rim of her champagne flute. "So, have you been doing any more modeling?" she asked. "I really liked that perfume thing you did."

Serena winced and took a gulp of champagne. Two months ago, the designer Les Best had asked her to star in the advertising campaign for his new perfume, and he'd even wound up naming the perfume Serena's Tears. In the ad Serena stood crying on a wooden footbridge in Central Park, wearing a yellow sundress in the dead of winter. Contrary to popular belief, the tears on her cheeks were entirely real. The ad had been shot the very moment Blair's dreadlocked vegan stepbrother, Aaron Rose, had decided to break up with her; the very moment the tears began to fall.

"Actually, I think I might try acting next," she replied.

Jenny nodded eagerly. "I just love how you look so *real* in that ad. Like, of course you look amazing, but not, like, air-brushed or made up or anything."

Serena giggled. "Oh my God, I was wearing *so* much makeup—you know that gross beige stuff they smear all over your face? And they totally airbrushed out my goosebumps. I was freezing my butt off!"

The lights over the bar went out for a second and everybody

screamed. Then they came on again. Jenny remained composed, eager to give the impression that she attended out-of-control parties like this all the time.

"Honestly," Serena declared, relieved to take a break from ruminating over her uncertain future. "Anyone can model. As long as you have the right look for the shoot."

"I guess," Jenny replied doubtfully. It was easy for Serena to say that anyone could model when she was endowed with giraffe-like legs, a gorgeous face, amazing dark blue eyes, and long, luxurious, natural blond hair. "But how do you know if you have the right look?"

"You go to something called a go-see," Serena explained. She polished off her champagne and pulled a pack of Gauloises cigarettes from her gold lamé Dior clutch. Within seconds the bartender zipped over to refill her glass and light her cigarette.

You know what they say: Beauty = Convenience.

"Listen, if you're interested, I can ask around and hook you up with some people I know," Serena offered.

Jenny stared up at her with huge brown eyes, unsure if she had misunderstood. It was so exactly what she'd wanted Serena to say, it was almost too good to be true. "You mean to model? *Me?*"

Just then Serena was distracted by a moan from behind her. "Um, you guys," she called over her shoulder to Vanessa and Dan. "There are suites and stuff downstairs, you know."

"I always thought I was way too short," Jenny insisted, worried that Serena was losing her train of thought.

"No way. You'll be great," Serena assured her. "I'm going to call some people, and then I'll e-mail you. Okay?"

"Really?" Jenny cried giddily. She couldn't believe this was happening. She was going to be a model! She set her champagne flute down on the bar. But now there was so much work to do. Manicure, pedicure, eyebrow shaping, mustache waxing, maybe even those henna highlights she'd always wanted.

"Aren't you going to finish it?" Serena asked, pointing at Jenny's glass.

Jenny shook her head, suddenly feeling completely unprepared. "I have to go home and get ready," she faltered. Then she stood on tiptoe and kissed Serena on the cheek. "Thank you. Thank you *so, so much*!"

Serena smiled down at the younger girl benevolently. So her best friend was mad at her and she wasn't in love? At least she could take pleasure in helping Jenny out.

As soon as Jenny left, three junior guys from Riverside Prep crowded behind Serena's bar stool, daring each other to ask her downstairs to one of the hotel suites with them.

"Man, is she hot. How come she doesn't have a boyfriend?" one of them murmured.

"Why don't you ask *her*?" his friend responded.

"Why don't *you*?" said the third guy.

But they were either too stupid, too chicken, or too humbled by Serena's beauty and supposed intelligence even to come close. Serena picked up the remains of Jenny's champagne and poured it into her glass.

It's no fun being beautiful when even losers won't talk to you.

they just wanna take their clothes off

"I can't believe this is happening," Vanessa breathed for the thirtieth time that night. She and Dan hadn't stopped kissing since he'd walked up to her in the bar and kissed her neck, and now they were tearing each other's clothes off in one of the Pier Hotel suites downstairs. She wanted to tell him how much she'd missed him and how stupid it was that they'd stopped talking. And even though sex in a hotel suite this close to graduation was tacky and clichéd, it felt like the best way.

The rooms in the Pier had round windows looking out onto the Hudson, wrought-iron anchors hanging from the walls, and sea green carpeting. The complimentary soap, shampoo, and body lotion in the bathroom were all seaweed-based, and the bed linens were a light, oceanic blue. Brushed-steel ceiling fans spun round and round from the ceilings, cooling off what was turning out to be a very hot night.

Dan yanked his belt out of his jeans and sent it snaking across the room. He was drunk with happiness and horny as hell. Bounding onto the bed, he jumped up and down on it a few times. "Whoo!" he shouted. "Whoo-hoo!"

Vanessa grabbed him around the knees and he fell down

on top of her, grappling with her shirt and yanking it off over her head.

"Dude! I survived!" some drunken doofus shouted. Next door, a bunch of guys in Bowdoin and Bates T-shirts were playing stupid drinking games while they watched the Nets game on TV.

"If we lived together, we could do this every day," Dan realized out loud as he watched Vanessa unhook her black lace bra.

Vanessa tossed the bra on the floor and crossed her arms over her bare chest. "Did you ask your dad?"

"Yup," Dan replied happily. "He said okay. But if my grades slip and if I don't have dinner with him and Jenny at least twice a week, I have to move back home." He pulled Vanessa's arms away and dove headfirst into her chest. Vanessa hugged his shaggy head and closed her eyes. She'd only drunk a Coke that night, but the bed was still spinning. She and Dan were in love again. They were moving in together. They might even go to NYU together. It was almost too perfect to believe.

And how often does anything ever stay that perfect?

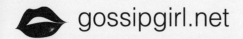 gossipgirl.net

Disclaimer: All the real names of places, people, and events have been altered or abbreviated to protect the innocent. Namely, me.

hey people!

Love how half the senior class is absent from school today. I also wanted to point out something you may have missed during last night's debauchery. Someone—actually a known-him-since-kindergarten friend of ours—was conspicuously absent from last night's proceedings. Here's why.

The dude who got in NOWHERE

He's always been so cocky about everything, no one had the slightest doubt he'd get in wherever he wanted to go. It never occurred to any of us that his cockiness might offend his teachers so much that they refused to give him recommendations; that his over-the-top I'm-a-male-runway-model style of dressing and suggestions that his family buy the school he decided to attend outright might turn interviewers off; that he was too cocky or too lazy or both to take the SAT more than once; or that he'd send with his applications a videotape of himself overacting in an interschool musical that he didn't even star in, instead of an application essay.

And so he was rejected. Not four or five times, but nine. *Nine rejections*. Ouch! Even the worst scumbag deserves some sympathy for that. But I'm sure he'll find a way to wheedle his way in somewhere. He always does.

Your e-mail

 Dear GG,
I'm an administrator at a prestigious East Coast university and I'm traveling to New York this weekend to meet a prospective

student. Our university wants him to attend next fall, so it's mandatory that I make a good impression. I hope you don't mind my asking, but what do you value most in a school? More important, what should I wear this weekend?
—adminchik

Dear adminchik,
I did enough college interviewing not to want to take your questions seriously if I don't have to. What are the fries like in your school's dining halls? If you ask me, that's pretty important. As for what to wear while you're wooing this highly desirable applicant? Orange is the new black.
—GG

Sightings

N escorting **B** home from **True West**, while the rest of us were only just getting the party started. **S** dancing by herself at the aforementioned party—although I'm pretty sure that group of guys behind her wanted to think they were dancing with her. **J** loading up on nail polish, hair-removal kits, and henna at the twenty-four-hour Duane Reade on Broadway. **V** and **D** stumbling out of the **Pier Hotel** *this morning*, just in time for school. **C**, with his monkey, drinking alone on the terrace of his **Sutton Place** apartment. We might even feel sorry for him if he weren't so impossible to feel sorry for.

Oops, that's the bell. More later!

You know you love me,

gossip girl

see j bounce

Jenny had always been lauded for her excellent calligraphy and detailed, accurate copies of the major works of classic artists. The handy thing about being artistic and a good copier was that she could forge notes, like this morning's note from her dad about a supposed "allergist appointment" downtown. She sniffled grotesquely as she handed it to her math teacher, Ms. Hinckle. In the back of the room, Elise tucked her straw-thick blond hair behind her ears and pretended not to eavesdrop.

"Next time, try to schedule your appointments *after* school," Ms. Hinckle instructed, dropping the note on her desk. She waved Jenny away. "Now shoo."

"Thanks," Jenny responded sheepishly. Ms. Hinckle was old and treated all of the girls like her grandchildren, baking them oatmeal cookies and making them Christmas cards and caramel apples. Jenny felt kind of bad taking advantage of the kindly teacher, but her career was at stake. This was important!

The go-see Serena had e-mailed her about was in a photographer's studio on West Sixteenth Street. A bunch of tall skinny girls with pouty lips and blond hair were smoking cigarettes on the sidewalk downstairs. *Models,* Jenny thought, trying not to feel intimidated.

She rang the buzzer for the third-floor studio and was buzzed into a dark space that looked like some sort of loading dock with a corrugated-steel-lined freight elevator. Jenny stepped onto the elevator and pressed 3, trying not to feel as terrified as she actually did.

"Hello?" A tall, pointy-chinned woman wearing a white patent leather beret, black leather short shorts, and white knee-high suede boots greeted Jenny as she stepped off the elevator. "Are you lost?"

Jenny realized she probably should have changed out of her Constance uniform, but it was too late now. "I'm here for the go-see?" She still wasn't even sure what a go-see was exactly, but it certainly sounded cool.

"Oh." The woman looked her up and down. "May I see your book?"

Jenny glanced down at her book bag. "My book?"

The woman gave her the once-over again, and pointed to an empty chair between two bored-looking blond models. "Sit down. I'll call you when he's ready." Then she stepped behind a white screen where Jenny could see a camera flash flashing and the shadows of bodies moving around the room. Suddenly a cacophony of hysterical laughter bounced off the studio's pounded tin ceilings, giving Jenny the shivers.

She glanced at the girl next to her. The girl was chewing gum, her eyelids drooping heavily like she'd been up all night. Jenny looked away and tried to make her eyelids droop in the same cool, affected way, but her eyeballs kept rolling back in her head. More *Night of the Living Dead* than cool, bored model.

The woman in the beret came out from behind the screen. "You." She pointed at Jenny.

Jenny blushed and glanced apologetically at the other girls who'd gotten there before her. Then she followed the woman behind the screen.

The screened-off part of the studio had brick walls painted white and a wood floor. In the center of the room was an antique-looking red velvet chaise lounge, and around the chaise lounge spotlights on tripods and silver reflective screens were set up.

"Take off your sweater and lie down," a stocky man with a blond goatee ordered, already squinting at her through a huge Polaroid camera.

Her heart pounding, Jenny put down her bag and folded her cardigan on top of it. Then she sat down on the edge of the red velvet chaise lounge, ashamed of how pale and knobbly her bare knees looked in the harsh light. "Lie down?"

"On your back," the photographer directed, kneeling in front of her only a few feet away.

Lie on her back? She couldn't possibly, not in the only moderately supportive cotton bra she was wearing. What if that horrible thing happened with her boobs, where each enormous breast oozed over her ribcage and into her armpits, causing her to look completely deformed?

She scooted back on the chaise and propped herself up on her elbows in a position she decided was comparable to lying down.

It also made her boobs stick out even farther than they already did.

"Good enough," the photographer muttered, slapping the Polaroids he'd already taken down on the floor and crawling toward her to take some more.

Jenny squeezed her legs together so he wouldn't be able to

see her underwear. "What kind of expression should I make?" she asked timidly.

"Doesn't matter," the man answered as he slapped down more film. "Just keep your shoulders back and your chin up."

Jenny's arms were beginning to tremble with strain, but she didn't care. The photographer seemed to like her. He was treating her like a real model.

"All right. We're done," he said finally, standing up. "What's your name anyway?"

"Jennifer," Jenny answered. "Jennifer Humphrey."

The man nodded at the woman in the beret and she jotted something down on her clipboard.

"May I see the pictures?" Jenny asked, pointing at the Polaroids lined up on the wood floor. Each one was covered with a black piece of film paper that had to be peeled away to see the image.

"Sorry, honey, those are mine," the photographer told her with an amused smile. "I want to see you here next Sunday. Ten A.M. Got it?"

Jenny nodded eagerly and slipped on her sweater. She wasn't completely sure, but it sounded like she'd just been hired as a model for a photo shoot!

Or at least some *part* of her had been hired.

"So what was the go-see for?" Serena asked when Jenny saw her at peer group during lunch later that day. "I'm sorry I couldn't find out more info. My model friends are pretty lame that way."

Jenny put her hand over her mouth. "I totally forgot to ask. But it was so great. Everyone was really nice to me, like I was a real model and everything."

"Okay, but you should find out at the shoot what it's for,"

Serena advised. "One girl I know thought she was doing a gum commercial and it turned out it was for maxipads. I guess she got confused between Carefree and Stayfree."

Jenny frowned. Maxipads? No one had said anything about maxipads.

"And don't let the stylist dress you in anything you're not comfortable with. I know that Les Best ad is good, but come on, a sundress in February? I was sick for like three weeks afterwards," Serena added.

The rest of the ninth-grade girls in peer group giggled politely. They loved hearing Serena's modeling stories, but they were superjealous of Jenny and didn't want to encourage her. How come the shortest girl in the class, the one with curly, boring brown hair and those ridiculously huge breasts, was now, like, a *model*? It made no sense.

"I bet it's for a plus-size bra catalog and she's too stupid to know," Vicky Reinerson whispered to Mary Goldberg and Cassie Inwirth

"I'm sure it's just for something basic, like orange juice," Cassie assured Jenny, trying to keep a straight face.

Elise was jealous, too, but she was trying hard not to show it. "Where's Blair?" she asked Serena in an effort to change the subject.

Blair was Serena's peer group co-leader. Serena shrugged. "I don't know. She's kind of mad at me right now."

Mary, Cassie, and Vicky nudged one another under the table. They loved being the first to find out about Serena and Blair's fights.

"I heard Blair didn't get into *any* of the colleges she applied to. Her dad's sending her to France right after graduation so she can work for him," Mary announced.

Serena shrugged again. She knew from experience how

stories got distorted and how quickly rumors spread. The less she said, the better. "Who knows what she'll do."

Jenny was still mulling over the maxipad issue. Did she really mind if the photo shoot next weekend was for something uncool, like frozen fat-free TV dinners or zit cream? At least it was a start. How else was she going to get discovered?

"Stop being so paranoid," Elise hissed at her, even though they weren't even supposed to be talking to each other. Ever since they'd become friends two months ago, Elise had had the uncanny ability to read Jenny's mind.

Talk about annoying.

Jenny glanced at Serena. The ethereally pretty senior had once had an unmentionable part of her body photographed by a pair of famous photographers, and the picture had wound up on the sides of buses and on top of taxis all over the city. It was one of the things that made Serena the coolest girl in the entire city, or maybe even the universe! A maxipad ad was the same kind of thing.

Sort of.

the stuff no one needs to know

"Forget your tender breasts, your swollen ankles, your stretch marks. Imagine your buttocks are balloons that are being deflated. Let go. Breathe *ouuut*."

Blair refused to imagine any such thing. It was bad enough lying on the floor with a bunch of pregnant women in their stinky stocking feet, all moaning like overfed cows— there was no need to degrade the situation even further by involving her buttocks.

On the floor to her right, Blair's mother giggled. "Isn't this fun?"

A blast.

Blair felt like hitting her. She'd taken a "personal day" and stayed home from school, too upset about being wait-listed at Yale to face her classmates, especially Serena. But after six hours of *Newlyweds* reruns, an entire carton of Häagen-Dazs fat-free chocolate sorbet, and now *this*, she wished she'd gone to school.

"All right. Now that the partners have had a moment to relax, it's time for them to get to work. Remember, it takes a team to make a baby!"

Eleanor's trendy-with-the-Upper-East-Side-set birth class

"coach" was a yoga-slim, frizzy-haired former nurse named Ruth, who taught the class in her ultramodern Fifth Avenue penthouse. Ruth was married to a newly successful appliance designer, meaning that he designed washing machines, refrigerators, and dishwashers that looked like spaceships and cost as much as cars. They had five children, including a set of fraternal twins, and every once in a while one of the children would wander through the living room to get something from the enormous chrome fridge in the kitchen without even batting an eye at all the pregnant women sprawled on the floor.

They'll probably all turn into psychologically disturbed gynecologists, Blair thought.

Ruth hitched up her weird black-and-white two-tone Yohji Yamamoto yoga pants, crouched on the floor, and scrunched up her face until she looked like a baboon trying to expel a whole banana tree from its ass. "Remember the stages of labor we went over in the beginning of class? This is the face of the third stage. Very antisocial. Later on, when the epidural has worn off and you begin to push? Forget about it. That's when you start shouting at your husband to fuck the prenup. Babies may be pretty, but there's nothing pretty about having them. That's why they call it *labor*."

Blair raised herself up on her elbows. Didn't they have more technologically advanced ways of doing this nowadays? Couldn't they just, like, *laser* the baby out?

"Now it's time for a treat. Ladies, keep relaxing on the floor. Partners, kneel down at their feet, where you belong. Now, ladies, get ready for a *fabulous* foot massage!"

All the other partners happened to be the women's husbands, not their seventeen-year-old daughters. Husbands were supposed to give foot massages. It was part of the job. Daughters weren't.

Blair stared at her mom's feet. They looked sort of like hers, except they were encased in skin-colored knee-high socks. Just the thought of touching them made Blair gag.

"Start working on the right heel. Cradle the foot in one hand and use your thumbs. Don't be afraid to dig in. She's been carrying two people around all day. Her feet are tough!"

Gingerly, Blair picked up her mother's right foot. One thing was certain: After each of these birth classes she was going to buy an extremely expensive pair of Manolos and charge them to her mother's credit card. She would also need a series of heavy-duty spa treatments to rid herself of the memories of all this touchy-feeliness and birth talk, never mind the foot odor.

"Now rest her foot on your chest and drum your fingers from the big toe up to the knee. I know it sounds odd, ladies, but it feels wonderful."

The husbands started drumming. They were really getting into it.

"I have to go to the bathroom," Blair announced, letting her mother's foot fall with a thud to the flokati-wool-carpeted floor.

"Why don't you use the twins' bathroom? It's just down that hall, on the right," Ruth said, coming over to take Blair's place.

"Ahh," Eleanor moaned as Ruth began to drum her fingers over her foot.

The bathroom was large and modern, like the rest of the house, but it was cluttered with bottles of Clearasil and assorted hair products. On the floor was a silver plastic litter box that looked like it had been designed by Ruth's husband, and bits of cat litter were scattered all over the tiles. Blair wasn't sure where Kitty Minky's litter box was located in her family's penthouse, but certainly not in her bathroom. How unsanitary!

She stood at the sink and ran the tap, staring at her reflection in the toothpaste-spattered mirror. Her thin lips were turned down at the corners, and her small blue eyes were hard and angry-looking. Her short brown hair was growing more slowly than she would have liked and was in a stage of styleless droopiness. She lifted up her shirt and examined her body. Her chest looked small, and her stomach was a little soft after not playing tennis all winter. Not that she was fat or anything. But maybe if she'd gone out for the swim team and stayed in shape, Yale would have wanted her and she would have already had sex with Nate and her life would be great instead of—

Suddenly the bathroom door swung open and Ruth's thirteen-year-old twins, a boy and a girl with braces and frizzy red hair like their mother, stood staring at Blair. The girl was wearing a gray pleated Constance Billard uniform. Blair let her shirt drop.

"We're looking for our cat," the girl said.

"Are you a lesbian?" the boy asked. The twins giggled in unison. "Because if you are, then how did you get pregnant?" continued the boy.

Excuse me?

Blair reached for the door and slammed it in their faces, careful to lock it this time. Then she flipped the lid down on the toilet seat and sat down. A worn copy of *Jane Eyre* was lying on the floor and she picked it up. Blair had read the book twice. Once on her own when she was eleven and once in ninth-grade English. Now she reread the first few pages, feeling very much like Jane herself—locked away, tortured by her family, her great intelligence and sensitivity completely underappreciated. If only the bathroom had some sort of escape route—a trapdoor to the street. She would take a cab straight to the airport, catch a plane to England or even Australia, change her name, get a job as a waitress or a governess, fall in love with her boss just like Jane, get married, and live happily ever after.

But first she had to wash away the disgusting odor of pregnant woman foot that seemed to have permeated her skin. Without stopping to think about what she was doing, Blair closed the book, stood up, and turned the tap on in the bath. She emptied a capful of Kiehl's cucumber body wash into the water, took off her clothes, and got in. There. Closing her eyes, she envisioned herself lying on an Australian beach in that shell-pink-and-navy-blue-plaid Burberry bikini she'd almost bought last weekend, watching her hot husband surf the Pacific. At sunset they'd sail out into the horizon in their yacht, drink champagne and eat oysters, and then have sex right on deck, his green eyes glittering in the moonlight. Green eyes . . .

Blair sat up in the tub. Nate! She didn't need to run away after all, not when she still had Nate. Her cell phone was sticking out of the back pocket of her jeans where they lay crumpled on the floor next to the tub. She grabbed it and dialed Nate.

"Whassup?" he asked, sounding stoned.

"Will you still love me even if I don't go to Yale?" Blair purred as she lay back in the bubbles.

"'Course I will," Nate responded.

"Do you think I'm fat and out of shape?" she asked, kicking one naked foot out of the water and then the other. Her toes were painted burgundy.

"Blair," Nate scolded her. "You're the opposite of fat."

Blair smiled and closed her eyes. She and Nate had had this conversation a thousand times before, but each time it always made her feel better about herself.

"Hey, are you taking a bath or something?" he asked.

"Uh-huh," Blair opened her eyes and reached for the bottle of body wash. "I wish you were here."

"I could come over," Nate offered hopefully.

If only she were actually home in her own bathtub.

"Sweetheart?" Eleanor Waldorf's voice called through the door. "Are you okay in there?"

"I'm fine!" Blair yelled back.

I'm just lying in my mother's birth class instructor's tub, having phone sex with my boyfriend.

"Well, don't forget there are a lot of pregnant women out here with overactive bladders!"

Thanks for the reminder.

"Damn, I gotta go," Nate said. "All these college lax coaches are calling me. They're coming down this weekend to watch me play."

Notice that he was careful not to mention *which* colleges.

"Well, I'm going down to Georgetown early tomorrow morning, but I'll call you from there, okay?" Blair clicked off and, with a rush of water, rose to her feet and dried herself off with one of the fluffy white towels she found folded in a stack on a shelf beside the tub. Then she pulled her clothes back on and ran her fingers through her damp hair. Her reflection in the mirror looked more vibrant now, and she smelled fresh and cucumber-clean. Maybe it was the bath, or the pick-me-up talk with Nate, but she felt like a whole new person.

Outside in the hallway, pregnant women were milling around eating goat-cheese-and-olive pizzettes delivered from

Eli's. Blair lingered by the door, waiting impatiently as Eleanor chatted with Ruth about Ruth's husband's refrigerator designs.

Ruth's twin daughter, the one in the Constance Billard uniform, walked over, carrying a white Himalayan cat.

"This is Jasmine," the girl said.

Blair smiled tightly and tightened the posts on her diamond stud earrings.

"Are you having a nervous breakdown?" the girl persisted. "I heard you had to drop out of school."

It was no secret how fast rumors flew around school and beyond. By Monday the braces-wearing, redheaded wretch would have told every soul who would listen how Blair Waldorf was looking at her chest in the bathroom at her house, or probably much worse. In a way Blair was actually looking forward to this weekend's trip to Georgetown. At least no one would know her, and she would be treated with the decency and respect she deserved.

"Mom!" she called harshly. "It's time to go."

And, just as Blair predicted, as soon as the door closed behind her, that evil twin raced to her room to log onto the computer, and the IMs began to fly.

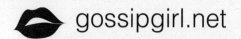 gossipgirl.net

Disclaimer: All the real names of places, people, and events have been altered or abbreviated to protect the innocent. Namely, me.

hey people!

Honesty is overrated

You know how everyone is always talking about how honesty is the best policy and how the only true relationship is an honest, open one? Well, I think that's crap. Not that I think lying is cool. Just that sometimes the less said, the better. I mean, how interesting can you be when you have no secrets? Where's the mystery? The element of surprise? Admit it, it's exciting when your boyfriend goes away for the weekend and you have no idea what he's been up to. You like it when that guy you have a crush on has a party but keeps to himself most of the time or leaves the room to make a mysterious phone call. Isn't it more interesting to imagine that everyone you know leads a double life?

And face it, if what we really wanted was honesty, we wouldn't talk so much trash about each other and thoroughly enjoy it, would we?

Your e-mail

 Dear GG,
It sounds strange, but my mom teaches childbirth classes in our living room, and this senior girl from my school was there last night with her mom, who is like way too old to be having a baby. Anyway, the girl like locked herself in the bathroom for like an hour and then came out all wet. Everyone in my class is so scared of her and thinks she's so cool, but now I know she's just crazy. No wonder she didn't get into college.
—newsworthy

A: Dear newsworthy,
You said she's a senior? Babe, we're ALL crazy.
—GG

Q: Dear GG,
My cousin goes to Yale and works as a tour guide for prospective students. He was told there is no wait list at Yale. They just send out the letters to meet some national quota or something.
—drea

A: Dear drea,
Eek. That sounds scary enough to be true.
—GG

Sightings

D drinking farewell coffee in a diner on **Broadway**. **J** practicing the runway-model strut down the center aisle of the Seventy-ninth Street crosstown bus. **S** catching the U.S. Air shuttle to **Boston**. Guess she's taking this decision-making thing pretty seriously. **B** chugging down one of those little bottles of vodka on her flight to DC—psyching herself up for **Georgetown**. **V** chucking out a GIRLS ONLY sign that she stole from a bathroom in a **Williamsburg** bar. **C** and his dad boarding their private jet. On their way to convince some gullible institution to take him next fall? Dad was carrying a briefcase—let's just imagine it was full of money.

Remember people, we've got almost three weeks to decide which school we want to go to. Let's use the time wisely. Wink, wink. You know I will!

You know you love me,

gossip girl

geeky harvard host steals *s*'s heart

Serena stepped out of her Logan Airport limo and tripped down the flagstone path to the Harvard admissions office, her body buzzing with caffeine from the huge Starbucks cappuccino she'd drunk during the flight. It was a sunny spring morning—cooler than in New York—and Cambridge was bustling with street vendors and hip, bohemian-looking students, hanging out on benches and drinking coffee. She wondered how Harvard had earned its serious and intimidating reputation when it seemed so relaxed and *un*intimidating.

Her tour guide was waiting for her just inside the door. Tall and dark-haired, with silver-wire-rimmed spectacles—the perfect geekily handsome intellectual. "I'm Drew," he said, holding out his hand.

"I already love it here," Serena gushed as she shook his hand. She had a tendency to gush when she was nervous, even though she wasn't exactly nervous, just over-caffeinated.

"I can give you the standard two-hour tour, or maybe it would be better if you tell me what you want to see," Drew offered. His eyes were light brown, and he was wearing a beige cotton cable-knit sweater and olive green corduroys that were so perfectly creased, Serena could picture him getting the package from J. Crew that his mom had had sent for him and putting the clothes on right out of the box. She liked it when boys paid attention to fashion, but it was almost more appealing when a boy looked hot *despite* his nerdy mom-just-bought-me-this outfit.

"I'd really like to see your room," she said, without even stopping to think about how it sounded. Actually, it was true. She really did want to see what the dorms were like.

Drew blushed and Serena blushed back at him. And all of a sudden it hit her—she'd gone to an all-girls school since first grade. All girls for twelve years straight. College was going to be full of *boys*. Boys all day, every day. *Boys, boys, boys.*

Whoopee!

"Are you hungry?" Drew asked. "The dining hall in my dorm actually has pretty decent food. I could take you through one of the bigger libraries and then we could walk over and get lunch and check out the dorm rooms. It's a coed dorm, so . . ." He blushed again and pushed his glasses up on his nose.

"Perfect," Serena breathed.

Drew led her out of the admissions office and down a long walkway that cut through Harvard Yard. The greener-than-green grass was crawling with students playing Frisbee or reading books. A professor corrected papers under a maple tree.

"This is Widener, the humanities library," Drew said as Serena followed him up the building's stately steps. "I'm a music-chemistry double major, so I don't really spend much time in here," he explained, holding the door open for her. They stepped inside the quiet, cool space, and

Drew pointed to a locked glass case standing against the far wall. "They have a pretty amazing collection of original manuscripts here. You know, ancient Greek papyri and stuff."

Papyri?

Drew stood patiently with his hands in the pockets of his neatly creased corduroys, waiting for her to ask questions about the library. But Serena was too absorbed in *him*. She'd already decided Drew was cute, but a boy who used words like *papyri* with a completely straight face was completely irresistible!

She twirled a strand of blond hair around her finger and stared up at the library's ceiling as if fascinated by its design. "You're a music major? Do you play an instrument?"

Drew looked down at the floor and muttered something inaudible.

She took a step closer. "Sorry?"

He cleared his throat. "The xylophone. I play xylophone, in the orchestra."

And she'd thought the xylophone was just a toy instrument invented so there'd be at least one English word that began with the letter *x*! Serena clapped her hands together in delight. "Can I hear you play?"

Drew smiled hesitantly. "I have practice at three, but I'm only just learning. You probably wouldn't want to stick around—"

Serena had ordered a car to drive her out to Providence that afternoon to check out Brown. Her brother, Erik, went there and was going to take her around campus for once instead of just getting her drunk with his roommates in his off-campus house. Still, it was only Erik. He'd understand if she was late.

When you're seventeen and blond and beautiful, you can always be late.

"Of course I'll stick around." She took hold of Drew's arm and pulled him out the library door. "Come on, I'm starving!"

Who needed libraries full of papyri when Harvard had so much more to offer?

b stands out at g-town

"My name is Rebecca Reilly and I'll be your host this week-end. Here's a name tag and a map and a whistle. Please wear the name tag and keep the map and whistle with you at all times."

Blair stared at the short, perky, fake blond girl in front of her. She had nothing against perkiness per se. She her-self even resorted to perkiness when she was trying to get a designer like Kate Spade to donate the gift bags for one of the big benefit parties she chaired, or when she needed a teacher to let her out early for a Chloé sample sale. But genuine perkiness among your *peers* was just plain sad and desperate.

"A whistle?" Blair repeated.

The entire plane ride down she'd been building this trip up as a big ego boost. She'd spend the day with some geeky tour guide who'd make her feel sophisticated and intelligent in comparison. Later on she'd get a room at the DC Ritz-Carlton or some equally grand hotel and spend the night soaking in her own private hot tub, quaffing champagne and indulging in more phone sex with Nate.

"Georgetown gives all its women students whistles. We

have a very strong women's advocacy group here. And there have been no campus rapes or stalkings in the past two years!" Rebecca announced in her southern twang. She beamed up at Blair through thick, blue-mascaraed lashes. Her permed, bleached-blond hair smelled of Finesse hair products, and her white leather Reeboks were so new, they looked like they'd never been worn outside the mall.

Blair flicked a stray hair off the sleeve of her new pink Marni suit jacket. "I need to book a hotel room for tonight—"

Rebecca grabbed her arm. "Don't be silly, sugar. You're staying with me and my girls. We have a quad that's just *deeelish,* and you have absolutely *the bestest* ever timing, because tonight we're having our girls-only Southern Belles *partay!*"

Hello? Since when was girls-only *anyone's* idea of a partay?

"Great," Blair responded weakly. If only she'd thought to book a room in advance. She looked around at the other visitors being greeted by their hosts. Everyone, hosts and visitors alike, looked strangely similar to Rebecca. Like they'd all grown up in suburban mall towns where everyone was blond and happy and clean and uncomplicated. Blair felt like a dark-haired, pixie-cutted, stylishly dressed, cynical and jaded alien among them.

Actually, it was just the sort of ego boost she'd been looking forward to. *See, I am different and smarter and better than these girls,* she told herself. At least she'd never stooped to dyeing her naturally walnut-colored locks blond.

"Come on, let's start the tour!" Rebecca grabbed Blair's hand like they were four years old and pulled her out of the admissions house. Sun glistened on the Potomac River, and the spires of the university's ancient Jesuit chapel towered majestically from the hilltop. Blair had to admit that the old

Georgetown University campus was beautiful, and the town of Georgetown was way nicer and cleaner than New Haven. But it definitely lacked the unique, we're-the-smartest-kids-in-the-class air of Yale.

"Up ahead on your left you'll see a big modern structure. That's our architectural award–winning Lauinger Library, with the largest collection of . . ." Rebecca walked backwards ahead of Blair down a flagstone walkway, burbling boring facts about Georgetown. Blair ignored her, keeping her eyes focused on the human traffic crisscrossing the main campus. Boys and girls dressed head-to-toe in Brooks Brothers or Ann Taylor marched purposefully toward the library, their Coach bags bulging with books. Blair took schoolwork seriously, but it was Saturday. Didn't these people have anything better to do?

Rebecca stopped suddenly and pressed her palm against her forehead. "Sugar, I am *so* hungover. This walking backwards thing is getting me so dizzy, I might puke!"

Blair wanted to say something about how the entire situation made *her* want to puke, but then again, so did most situations. "Why don't we just sit down somewhere and have a . . . coffee," she suggested, pleased with how normal and friendly she sounded, when what she could really use was a very strong vodka martini.

Rebecca threw her arms around Blair's neck. "A girl after my own heart!" she squealed. "I'm absolutely *addicted* to caramel macchiatos, aren't you?"

Yuck.

It was only two o'clock. Coffee would have to do. "Is there someplace close by?"

Rebecca slipped her arm through Blair's. "There sure is!" She whipped out her pink-and-white sparkly Nokia phone.

"Just give me a minute to round up the girls. Why not get our Southern Belles part*ay* started earl*ay*?"

Blair grimaced and fingered the cell phone in her mint green Prada bubble bag. Already she was homesick for Nate. If only she'd borrowed the silver flask he carried around, then she'd at least have a memento of him, and a shot of vodka for her macchiato.

Rebecca looked up from the little telethon she was having with her friends. She held her hand over the mouthpiece. "They're in a bar already," she whispered, her cheeks flushing a perky, embarrassed pink. "It's down on M Street. Do you mind if we meet them there?"

"Okay," Blair agreed readily. Give her a cocktail and a cigarette and she could be happy in almost any company.

how badly do they want him?

"Dude, you never told me the coaches were all chicks," Jeremy Scott Tompkinson, one of Nate's best buddies, hissed as he sprinted past Nate to retrieve a long pass.

Nate twirled his lacrosse stick overhead and waited until Jeremy had overshot before stepping in to catch the pass himself. It was a show-off kind of maneuver, but it was effective. Besides, he was supposed to be showing off. He tossed the ball back to Jeremy, demonstrating his teamwork skills the way Coach Michaels had asked him to. Then the two boys ran back to center field together.

"The tall one's the Yale coach. The short one is the Brown admissions chick who interviewed me," Nate explained. "The Brown coach couldn't make it because of a game."

"But dude, they're all chicks!" Jeremy said again, his shaggy rock star haircut flapping around in the breeze as he jogged away. "No wonder you got in!"

Nate grinned to himself as he wiped the sweat from his brow. It might have been nice to believe he was completely oblivious to his perfection, but the truth was, he knew exactly how hot he was. He just wasn't an asshole about it.

From the sidelines the two women watched him intently.

Then Coach Michaels blew the whistle. "Gotta quit early today, boys!" the coach shouted, spitting into the grass. "Wife and I are celebrating our fortieth anniversary tonight." He tucked his gnarled hands into his forest green Lands' End windbreaker and nodded at Nate before spitting into the grass once more. "Come on, Archibald."

Nate followed the coach over to where the two university women were standing.

"It'd be great to have our own pitch," Coach Michaels told the women. He gestured at the stretch of Central Park grass where Nate's teammates were dismantling the goals. "But when you play in the city, you use what you've got."

As if they really had it rough.

On a bench nearby, four tenth-grade girls in green plaid Seaton Arms uniforms giggled and whispered to one another, their eyes fixed longingly on Nate.

"At least in the park you always have an audience," the Yale coach observed. She was tall and horsey-looking, with a mane of blond hair and a handsome, angular face. A street vendor was selling drinks and ice cream from a cart parked near the benches. She unzipped the front pocket of her navy blue backpack with the gray Yale bulldog decal on it. "Can I buy you two a Gatorade or something?"

"No thanks, ma'am. Gotta get home to the wife." Coach Michaels shook hands with the two women and then clapped Nate on the back. "He's a talented boy. Let me know if you have any questions."

The coach took off, and Nate whacked at the new spring grass with his lacrosse stick. "I better get home and shower," he mumbled, unsure of what the two women had planned. Brigid, his interviewer from Brown, was watching him expectantly. Brigid had left a message on his cell phone asking him to meet her in the lobby of the Warwick New York Hotel at five o'clock that afternoon to "discuss his options."

Whatever that meant.

The coach from Yale handed him a blue nylon sports bag with a big white leather *Y* embossed on it. "Compliments of the team," she said. "Your jersey and shorts and stuff are all in there. Jockstrap. Even socks."

Brigid's face fell. Guess she hadn't thought of that. "Are we still on for later?" she asked quickly. "I could buy you dinner." Her hair was strawberry blond, which Nate hadn't remembered from when he met her in October, and he wondered if she'd dyed it. Actually, she was a lot cuter than he remembered and he kind of liked that she hadn't tried to seduce him with a whole bag full of Brown sweatshirts and shit. Even if he decided to go to Yale, did he really need a Yale-issue jockstrap?

"I'll be there," he said. Then he held out his hand to the Yale coach. "Thanks for coming down."

But the coach wasn't giving up that easily. "How 'bout I take you to brunch around eleven tomorrow? I'm in the Hotel Wales on Madison—Sarabeth's is right downstairs. Their pancakes are wicked good."

Nate noticed the Yale coach had a seriously nice chest— big, but firm. She looked like one of those hot Olympic volleyball players. He slung the Yale bag over his shoulder. "Sure," he agreed. "Brunch sounds good."

It was kind of a head trip to be schmoozed this hard by two of the hardest-to-get-into colleges in the country, and it might be fun to see just how badly they wanted him.

upper west sider flies the coop

"Tell me honestly, is this obscene?" Jenny asked. Vanessa was perched on the edge of Jenny's bed filming her while she selected an outfit for her upcoming photo shoot. Vanessa was supposed to be helping Dan pack, but he'd discovered a notebook full of poems he'd written back when he was thirteen and was busy hunting for some recyclable poetic gem.

Good luck with that.

Jenny had psyched herself up to appear at the photo shoot without a bra, something she never did, at least not in public. Not only that, she'd decided to wear a light blue T-shirt that was kind of tight. "So, what do you think?"

"Yes, it's obscene," Vanessa replied matter-of-factly, careful to keep the camera focused above Jenny's shoulders so her ratings wouldn't go from PG-13 to NC-17.

"Really?" Jenny turned around to check out her butt in the mirror on the back of her closet door. Her new Earl jeans made her legs look so much longer than her other jeans did. It was a remarkable feat of engineering.

Vanessa panned around the room. It was a typical adolescent girl's room, decorated in pink and white, with a collage of pictures ripped out of fashion magazines tacked to the wall and a bookshelf strewn with teen fiction and half-dressed Barbies that never got thrown out. The art on the walls was definitely unique, though. A perfect replica of Klimt's *The Kiss*, an impressive copy of van Gogh's *Windmills*, and a stunning O'Keeffe-like poppy—all painstakingly painted by Jenny herself.

Vanessa panned back to her subject. "Why don't you try a black shirt?" she suggested. "And a bra."

Jenny's face fell. "It's that bad?"

Her dad appeared in her open doorway, the long pieces of his wiry gray hair pulled up on top of his head in one of Jenny's scrunchies. "Jesus, girl, put a sweater on or something," Rufus gasped. "What will the neighbors think?"

Jenny knew her dad was playing around, but it was pretty clear what the general consensus was. She pulled a sweatshirt out of her closet and pulled it on over her head. "Thanks, people. It's so nice to know you care," she said, glaring at her dad. "Any chance I could move into your place, too?" she asked Vanessa.

"Absolutely not," Rufus retorted. "Who will drink all the orange juice before I even get up in the morning? Who will fill up the butter compartment of the fridge with nail polish? Who will bleach my black socks pink?"

Jenny rolled her eyes. Her dad would be really lonely all by himself. And she didn't really want to live with Dan and Vanessa anyway. Not when they were practically married and everything. It would be way too weird.

All of a sudden Vanessa felt horribly guilty for taking Dan away from Rufus when Dan's mother had already left years ago to live in Prague with some baron or something. "We'll come over for dinner on weekends," she offered lamely. "Or you guys could come over and cook. Ruby has lots of great cooking stuff. Someone better teach me how to use it."

Rufus brightened. "We can have cooking tutorials!"

Vanessa fiddled with her camera lens, trying to get Rufus into the picture. "Mr. Humphrey, do you mind if I ask you some questions?" she asked.

Rufus sat down on the floor and pulled Jenny down next to him. "We love the attention!" he said and pinched his daughter in the side.

"Dad," Jenny whined, crossing her arms over her chest even though she was wearing the sweatshirt.

"So, how does it feel to have a son old enough to be going to college and moving out?" Vanessa asked.

Rufus tugged on his wiry, untamed salt-and-pepper beard. He was smiling, but his brown eyes were liquid and sad-looking. "If you ask me, he should have moved out a long time ago. American families spoil their kids. They should start school as soon as they can hold their heads up, and they should be out of the house by fourteen." He pinched Jenny's side again. "Right about when they start acting resentful toward their fathers."

"Dad," Jenny whined again. Then she brightened. "Hey, does this mean I can have Dan's room? It's like twice the size of mine."

Rufus frowned. "Let's not get ahead of ourselves," he grumbled. "He still needs a room." He cocked a wild eyebrow at Vanessa. "You might kick him out. He might even get kicked out of college!"

"But you just said—" Jenny started, and then stopped. Her father was always contradicting himself. She should have been used to it by now. "Anyway, once I get some modeling money, I can redecorate this room," she added.

Rufus rolled his eyes dramatically for the sake of the camera and Jenny punched him in the arm. Then Dan appeared in the doorway. He was wearing a Kelly green Lacoste polo shirt that his mother had sent him a few years ago. It was about three sizes too small and made him look like a golf-playing dweeb on crack.

"That shirt stays here," Vanessa ordered.

Dan chuckled, pulled the shirt off over his head, and tossed it into Jenny's trash basket.

"Hey," Jenny whined. "Use your own trash can."

"It's just a shirt. You can handle it," Dan growled back.

Then Jenny burst into a fit of giggles. Dan thought he was such a stud because he'd had a poem published in *The New Yorker* and had gotten into all those colleges, but without a shirt on he looked really puny, and wasn't it sort of lame that he did absolutely everything Vanessa told him to without question?

"I'll really miss you, Dan," Jenny sighed with pretend dolefulness.

Rufus pulled a packet of mini cigars out of his back pocket and passed them out to everyone without any explanation. Then he lit his and began to puff away. "Maybe it's for the best," he sighed.

Vanessa turned off her camera and rolled her unlit cigar around between her lips. It was hard not to feel guilty when Rufus looked so sad, but then again, she couldn't wait to have Dan all to herself, twenty-four hours a day, seven days a week. Her eyes were riveted on his pale, bony chest. It was the chest of a tortured artist. Her man.

"Ready to go?" she asked, grinning at him excitedly.

Dan grinned back. He still hadn't come down from his happy high, and he wasn't planning to anytime soon. "Ready," he responded gamely.

Let's just hope he packed some other shirts.

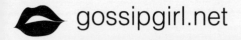

hey people!

Annoying Girl

You know who I mean. The one who thinks she's gorgeous and smart and every boy is in love with her. She shouts, "Me, me, me!" and waves her hand in the air whenever the teacher asks a question. She's the most self-righteous person in the room, but she's insecure about appearing too self-righteous, so she giggles a lot and acts stupid to hide her supposed genius. And she's the loudest, messiest drunk you've ever seen. Without her friends, she'd pass out in a puddle of sick on the bathroom floor or wind up going home with some sleazy older guy. But her friends always seem to take pity on her, and the next day she's bouncier than ever, smiling like nothing happened.

The thing about Annoying Girl is, whether we like it or not, we all have a little bit of her in us. That's why we love to hate her so much. She's our worst nightmare. I mean, how many times have you wanted to wave your hand in the air when you knew the answer, only stopping yourself because you didn't want to look like an idiot? And how many times have you wanted to just sit down in a boy's lap and start kissing him but didn't for fear he'd laugh in your face? In a way, Annoying Girl is us minus the insecurity. She's so fine with herself you want to slap her. But you also secretly wish you could be that obnoxious without any concern for what other people might think. Face it, people will always find reasons to hate us, especially if we're beautiful.

Though there is one particular blond girl who seems unable to do wrong. Not only did she get into every impossible-to-get-into college she applied to, she's already got all the guys at each of those schools lining up to talk to her.

Your e-mail

Q: Dear GG,
I heard there's this whole forgery scandal going on. Like you can pay someone to make you totally convincing acceptance letters to like, Princeton, or wherever, and there's nothing the schools can do about it because they are so real.
—wiz

A: Dear wiz,
You can buy anything these days, but if you weren't a good enough student to get into a school as hard as Princeton on your own merits, would you really want to fake it? I mean, eventually you might have to do some work!
—GG

Sightings

This just in: **S** and geeky-but-cute glasses-wearing **Harvard** boy feeding each other French fries in one of the Harvard dining halls. She's got her college selection criteria straight. Cute boys, check. Decent fries, check. **B** hanging with her new homegirls in a karaoke bar in **Georgetown**. She really is having a nervous breakdown! **N** doing some private drills with the leggy blond who coaches **Yale**'s lacrosse team. Nudge, nudge. As if he didn't already have enough secrets from **B**. Little **J** in that hole-in-the-wall bra shop in the Village where they take one look at you and tell you you're a totally different size than you thought. In her case, an *E*-cup! **V** and **D** in **Williamsburg**, grocery shopping together. Actually, they were fighting over whether to get spaghetti or a more interestingly shaped pasta—yup, married already.

Meanwhile, back at the ranch, I'm thinking of putting on a tracksuit and pretending to be a lacrosse coach. Who knows, I may get lucky!

Be good. You know I won't be.

You know you love me,

gossip girl

thirty seconds of true love

Serena held Drew's cheeks in her hands and blew steam into the lenses of his glasses. Then she rubbed it off with the tip of her perfectly shaped nose. "Promise me you'll come to New York?"

She'd spent the entire afternoon sitting right next to Drew in the pit during orchestra practice. The conductor had even let her play the timpani and the bells! Of course, she could hardly keep time watching Drew play xylophone. The way he closed his eyes and pursed his lips and tapped his feet as he played was beyond adorable. After practice he'd bought her a cappuccino in the coffee house, and they'd started to share a brownie. But by then Serena was so smitten she'd had to drag Drew back to his dorm room for a private xylophone lesson.

Uh-huh.

Not that she'd gotten him out of his neatly pressed J. Crew cords—he wasn't that kind of boy—but he definitely knew how to kiss. Now they lay entwined on his narrow bed, their clothes all rumpled and their hair matted to their heads. Serena wanted to stay that way for the rest of the weekend; unfortunately, she had to go.

Drew took off his glasses and cleaned them on his pillowcase.

He put them back on and cleared his throat. "So, do you think you'll decide to go here in the fall?"

"Definitely," Serena breathed. She nuzzled her head into his chest. "I don't know how I'm going to make it until then without you."

There were only two weeks left of Drew's sophomore year. Then he was off to Mozambique for the summer to study percussion.

Drew kissed her hair. "I'll come down and visit before I go, and I'll write every day while I'm gone."

Aw.

Serena closed her eyes and kissed him for a long, long time. It was dinnertime and the dorm was quiet. Then, all of a sudden, voices resounded in the hall outside as people returned to their rooms to do whatever it was people did after dinner at college—study, flirt with the hottie down the hall, study, hook up with the hottie down the hall, pretend to study, make cosmos, play strip poker, order pizza.

The door opened and Drew pulled away from her.

A redheaded boy wearing a red baseball hat and black basketball shorts stood in the doorway. "Hey. S'happening?" he said in a strong Massachusetts accent.

"Wade, Serena. Serena, my roommate Wade. Serena is from New York. She's on her way down to Brown," Drew explained, looking flustered.

Serena sat up and wiped her mouth.

"Just stopped by to check out Harvard," Wade observed in a mocking tone. "Guess you liked it okay."

Serena blushed even harder. She swung her feet to the floor and slipped them into her brown suede Calvin Klein flats. "I better go. My driver's been waiting for over an hour."

"I'll walk you," Drew offered. As soon as they were out of

the room and walking down the hall to the exit doors, Drew gave Serena's hand a little squeeze. "For the past two years Wade has given me shit about not having a girlfriend. I don't think he expected to see me with someone so . . ." He faltered and bit his lip, as if embarrassed by the stream of adjectives that was about to pour out of his mouth.

Mouthwateringly hot? Supremely bodacious? Superbly succulent? *Female?*

Serena grinned up at him as he held the door open for her, her cheeks pink with the rush of love. Drew didn't have to finish his sentence. She knew how he felt, because she felt exactly the same way about him.

A gray Lincoln town car was waiting at the bottom of the steps, ready to whisk her off to Providence. She wrapped her arms around Drew's neck, pressed her cheek against his, and inhaled in an attempt to absorb as much of him as possible. "I love you," she whispered in his ear before pulling away and running down the steps and into the car.

Drew raised his hand to wave good-bye and the car pulled away, leaving Serena smiling and crying and happier than she had felt in a long, long time. At long last she'd found true love.

A love that would last for at least thirty seconds.

b learns something at college

"Okay, so you want to hear something totally gross?" Forest, one of Rebecca's Georgetown roommates, asked the group.

Blair was seated around a table with Rebecca and her three roommates in the back of Moni Moni, a cheesy Georgetown karaoke bar. A tour bus full of nerdy-looking Hungarian men in tracksuits monopolized the karaoke machine, putting everything they had into "Staying Alive" by the Bee Gees. Blair and the other girls were drinking green kiwi-flavored frozen cocktails called Kiwi the Snowman while they pretended not to notice how obnoxious the so-called music was. The drinks were ridiculously strong, and they were having trouble stringing sentences together.

"I'm sure you're going to tell us, even if we don't want to know," Gaynor replied. Gaynor had black hair streaked with blond and a nose that was so severely pugged, Blair could see straight up it.

Not that she was really looking.

"Will you just tell us already?" Rebecca whined.

"Okay," Forest said slowly. She lit a cigarette and paused dramatically. Forest was Korean-American and had bleached-blond hair that would have looked so much better if she just let it be brown.

Not that Blair cared enough to say anything.

"So you know how Georgetown is supposed to be all about brotherly love and there are no fraternities and everything is supposed to be all uncompetitive and all? Well, I just found out that there's this underground lacrosse fraternity, and for orientation the older boys make the younger boys eat a cracker with their jizz on it. It's like this whole ritual thing. And if you, like, don't eat the cracker, you don't get on the team."

Everyone made a face, including Blair. Sometimes boys were just . . . gross. Except for Nate, who would never ever do anything remotely that disgusting.

"You're from New York City?" Fran piped up. Fran was only four-foot-eleven, weighed about eighty pounds, and spoke in a breathy whisper. Her skin was so transparent, Blair thought she could actually see Kiwi the Snowman pumping through her veins. "I've only been there once. I got food poisoning at a sushi restaurant and spent the whole week puking."

"As if you don't puke enough already," Forest quipped, suggesting that Fran's diminutive size was self-imposed.

"Do you know that guy Chuck Bass?" Gaynor asked Blair.

Blair nodded. Everyone knew Chuck, whether they liked it or not.

"Is it true he didn't get in *anywhere*?" Rebecca asked, crunching ice between her slightly bucked teeth.

"That seriously bites," Forest said, without a hint of sympathy.

Silently, Blair gulped of her drink. Since Georgetown was looking less and less appealing and she basically had no other options, she could almost sympathize with Chuck.

"Do you know Jessica Ward?" Rebecca asked. "She came here for a term and then transferred to BU?"

Blair shook her head. She didn't know Jessica, but she could see why she'd transferred.

"Do you know Kati Farkas?" Fran asked. "We went to camp together."

Blair nodded tiredly. The game was wearing thin. "She's in my class at Constance."

"What about Nate Archibald?" Gaynor asked. She nudged Forest's arm with her elbow and wiggled her eyebrows suggestively. "Remember him?"

Forest nudged her back. "Shut up," she snapped, looking pissed-off and sad at the same time.

Blair's hackles rose. "What about him?"

"He visited here once. And seriously, he was the biggest stoner ever. But I heard he got recruited for lacrosse at all the best schools, even Yale. I don't think he bothered to apply here. He didn't need to."

"Nate Archibald," Fran repeated. "We were all so in love with him," she giggled hoarsely. "Especially Forest."

"Shut up!" Forest snapped again.

Blair's stomach churned. The Hungarians were taking a stab at Eminem now. *Na, na, na, na, na. Na, na, na, na, na,* they rapped obnoxiously. She pushed away her drink. "Nate got into Yale? That's such a lie," she said, almost to herself. Then again, when it came to Nate, she never knew what to believe.

"Why would we lie to you? We don't even know you," Gaynor retorted bitchily.

Blair stared at her for a moment and then bent down to retrieve her purse from underneath the table. "I'll be right back," she announced, and then stumbled towards the bathroom.

n is for naughty

Brigid had interviewed Nate back in the fall, so she already knew he'd spent every summer since he was born sailing up in Maine. Because of this she assumed he liked lobster. And because she was supposed to lavish him with the best of everything in order to entice him up to Brown, she took him to the restaurant Citarella, where she'd preordered a giant broiled lobster for the two of them to share, along with a bottle of Dom Pérignon and a basket of pommes frites.

"I grew up in Maine," she explained, tugging on her pearls. "Camden. All my family ever did was sail and eat lobster."

The truth was, Nate thought lobster was sort of ridiculous, like some silly crustacean cartoon character that could dance on its tail and hold a microphone in its claw and sing and tell jokes and make people giggle. It certainly wasn't the sort of food he craved when he had the munchies.

Which was basically all the time.

"So." Brigid topped off her champagne flute, even though the waiter had just filled it. She'd changed into low-cut orange dress and was wearing sparkling lip gloss and mascara. Her strawberry blond hair was freshly brushed and she looked even cuter than she had earlier that day on the lacrosse pitch in the park. She fiddled nervously with the stem of her glass. "So, enough about me. Do you, um . . . ?" She bit her lip. "Do you have a girlfriend?"

Nate poked at his salad, smearing goat cheese all over the leaves. He was pretty sure Brigid's low-cut dress and flirtatious behavior went beyond her mission of getting him to matriculate at Brown. He suspected she had a crush on him. But she was still his Brown interviewer, and he wanted to make a good impression.

"Um. Sort of." he told her hesitantly. "I mean, sometimes we're together and sometimes we're not."

She seemed to like that answer. "Are you together now?"

Nate had always preferred beer to champagne but he gulped his wine Blair-style. In theory, he and Blair *were* together again, happily, hooray. But they hadn't exactly discussed the *terms* of their relationship. Did flirting with his Brown admissions officer really qualify as cheating?

Suddenly his phone rang and he whipped it out of his pocket, kicking himself for forgetting to turn it off before dinner. He glanced at the phone's little screen. Speak of the devil.

Nate's head was a little fuzzy from the six bong hits he'd done at Anthony Avuldsen's house before he came out. Speaking to Blair might knock some sense into him.

"Um, I should take this," he told Brigid. "Hey," he said into the phone.

"Hello," Blair responded coldly. "Before you say anything I just have to ask you a question."

Her voice was clipped, as if she was trying to use as few syllables as possible. Nate could tell she'd been drinking. "Okay."

"Tell me the truth. Did you apply to Yale?"

Oh, boy.

Nate grabbed his champagne and polished it off. *Fuck!* He cursed silently. *Fuck, fuck, fuck.* There was definitely no right answer. If he said yes, he was a bastard and a liar, and if he said no, he was a bastard and a liar.

Brigid was smiling at him expectantly, her lips all shiny and glossed. At least he could take comfort in the fact that Blair was miles away at Georgetown, and he was having dinner with his Brown interviewer, who was dying to see him naked. He decided to tell the truth.

"Yeah, I did. And I guess I got in."

Blair made a strange gurgling noise, and then Nate heard the distinct, familiar sound of her puking into a toilet. "Fuck you," she growled into the phone before hanging up.

Nate turned the phone off and tucked it into his pocket. The waiter arrived with the lobster. "Boy, does that look good," Nate said, his voice hollow.

"Do you want to share the tail?" Brigid asked, handling the steaming crustacean with practiced ease. She pointed at the stainless-steel claw-cracking tools the waiter had brought. "Or get started on a claw?"

What Nate really wanted was to do a few more bong hits and then eat a big bowl of Breyers chocolate ice cream while sitting comatose in front of *The Matrix,* which he'd already seen eighteen times.

Brigid put down the lobster. "Are you okay?"

He shrugged. "I think my girlfriend just broke up with me again."

Brigid's green eyes opened wide. "You poor thing." She motioned to the waiter. "Can we have this to go?" She pushed back her chair. "Come on. I'll buy you a beer and a cigarette."

Nate tried to tell himself that since Blair wasn't around to murder him right now he was basically safe and should enjoy the next twenty-four hours before she came back. He could even hook up with Brigid if he wanted to.

The thing was, he was sick of always breaking up with Blair when they both knew that they were supposed to be together for the rest of their lives. And unlike Blair, he didn't really care what college he went to. In fact, he'd be fine with not going to college at all for a couple of years. As far as he could tell, the only way to put himself and Blair back on a level playing field was to try and get his Brown and Yale acceptances revoked. And what better way to do that than to act like an asshole?

"Fuck it," Nate said under his breath. He stood up and helped Brigid into the denim jacket hanging on the back of her chair. His fingers brushed her neck as he pulled her hair out from underneath the collar. They were standing very close, and Brigid's breath smelled like Hawaiian Punch. "How badly does Brown want me?" he murmured into her ear.

Her green eyes opened wide. "Bad," she whispered unsteadily.

Her hotel room key was on the table. Nate picked it up and dropped it in his pocket.

"Bad," she whispered again.

The waiter handed Nate a plastic bag with the twenty-pound lobster wrapped up in foil inside it. He chucked it on the table and put his arm around Brigid's waist.

"Show me," he told her gruffly, disgusted with the sound of his voice.

Guess he wasn't talking about the lobster.

s takes the road less traveled

Only a half hour into their journey to Providence, Serena asked the driver to stop at a gas station. The convenience store was tiny and badly stocked, but she bought a Coke, a Twix bar, and a local newspaper just to have something to do while she was mooning over Drew. Outside, a boy was standing just beyond the pumps, holding up a sign that said BROWN. He was wearing faded jeans and a nice blue-and-white-striped button-down shirt, and docksiders without socks. On his back was a complicated purple-and-black backpack, the type people take on long hikes. His curly black hair looked clean and he seemed normal enough.

"Need a ride?" she called over.

The boy whipped his head around. "Me?"

Serena liked how big and wide open his brown eyes were. "I've got a driver to take us up there. Come on," she offered.

The boy grinned shyly and followed her to the car. He sat close to the door and put his backpack between them. A patch of the Italian flag was sewn onto it. Serena drank her Coke and pretended to read her newspaper. Then the boy pulled a drawing pad and pencil from out of his backpack and began to scribble away.

At first she thought it was homework or a letter, but then she yawned and let her head fall back against the seat back, surreptitiously taking a gander at what the boy was writing. Much to her surprise, he was sketching her. Her *hands*, to be exact.

"Do I get to keep that when you're done?" she asked.

The boy jumped, as if he thought he'd been really coy and secretive about the fact that he was drawing her. He closed his notebook and tucked the pencil behind his ear. "Sorry."

"That's all right." Serena stretched her arms over her head and then let her hands fall into her lap. "I'm in such a daze anyway. Go ahead. Keep drawing."

He opened his notebook again. "You don't mind?"

"Nope." After all, she was a professional model. She sat back and folded her hands the same way they'd been before. "Is this okay?"

"Mmm," the boy answered, his head bent over his work. He had dark olive skin and thick black curls and he exuded an odor of fresh mint.

Serena closed her eyes, trying to recall what Drew's hair was like. She remembered that his roommate Wade's hair was red. And Drew's was sort of . . . dark blond? Chestnut? She honestly couldn't remember. She opened her eyes again and glanced at the boy again. The back of his neck looked soft and brown. *If we had children, they'd have year-round tans and that sort of sandy blond-brown hair that's so pretty in the sun,* she mused. Then she looked away again, horrified. What was wrong with her? She didn't even know his name!

The boy looked up again. "Do you go to Brown?"

Serena kept her gaze fixed on the window. It was dirty and she could see his reflection in it. His black eyelashes were curly and his brown eyes were wonderfully soft, like Bambi's or something. "Not yet, but I might, next year."

Wait, wasn't she all about Harvard like five seconds ago?

"I hope so," he said quietly before turning back to his drawing.

Serena didn't know what had gotten into her, but she was totally turned on. *What if I just grabbed him and kissed him?* she wondered to herself. The driver was listening to some baseball game on the radio; he wouldn't even notice.

"You know, you would be a great artist's model," the boy told her. "You could sit for the figure-drawing classes at Brown. Professor Kofke is always looking for good models."

"Thanks. Actually, I have done some modeling," Serena began, but then shut herself up for fear of sounding like a brat.

The boy tucked his pencil behind his ear, studying his drawing. "It doesn't even matter to me whether a model is beautiful or not. Usually I only do hands."

Serena peered over his shoulder. He really did smell like mint. "You made my hands look much nicer than they are. Look at my thumbnail: I've chewed it to bits! And this one . . ." She held out her left pinky. "My poor cuticles!"

But the boy wasn't even looking. He unzipped a side pocket in his backpack, pulled out a piece of paper, and handed it to her.

Serena unfolded the piece of paper. It was a clipping ripped from a magazine. "Tighter Abs in Seven Days," the caption read.

"Turn it over," the boy told her.

She flipped the clipping over. On the back of it was the ad for Serena's Tears. There she was, crying in the snow in Central Park, wearing a yellow sundress.

"Is that really your name? Serena?" He asked, gazing at her with those Bambi eyes.

"Yes."

He took the clipping back. "I lied about only doing hands. I thought I was dreaming when you picked me up at the gas station back there. I've been painting you for two months. From this picture. I'm still not finished. It's in the studio, up at Brown." He folded up the clipping and tucked it into his backpack. Then he held out his hand. "I'm Christian."

Serena let her hand linger in his. She supposed she should have been freaked out, but instead she was more turned on than ever. "Would you mind showing me around a little when we get there?" she asked. "I'm supposed to meet my brother, but I'm already so late, he's probably already in a bar or something." Erik wouldn't mind if she blew him off. Brothers and sisters always blew each other off all the time. Besides, Christian could probably give her a much more thorough tour.

Yeah, you bet he could.

b joins exclusive g-town sisterhood

The Hungarians were gone, replaced by three women in Smithsonian Museum security uniforms singing Whitney Houston. *"And IeeeeIeeeI will always love you!"*

Talk about painful.

The moment she hung up with Nate, Blair went over to the bar and ordered a pitcher of pink grapefruit margaritas for the table.

"You guys saved my life," she told Rebecca, Forest, Gaynor, and Fran as she set the pitcher down. The girls' heads wobbled drunkenly in response. Blair sat down, lit a cigarette, took a drag, and then passed it to Rebecca. "I'm just glad I got you as a tour guide, and not some loser."

Rebecca passed the cigarette around, and the girls' lip glosses combined to make a smudgy plum-colored stain on the filter. "Last month Forest was taking this prospective student around—a guy. They got caught by the dean of students practically doing it in the laundry room. She got fired by admissions."

"Shut up," Forest whined, but she was smiling.

Blair tried to imagine what her visit would have been

like if her tour guide had been a guy, but knowing her luck, he'd have been a total geek. She stared at Forest, wondering if maybe she ought to say something about how Forest's bleached-blond hair looked cheap and slutty and no wonder the admissions office didn't want her to be a tour guide. But since she was drunk as a fish, she said something else entirely.

"So, are any of you still virgins?"

The four girls giggled and kicked each other under the table. Blair lit another cigarette, feeling slightly annoyed that she'd set herself up to admit that she was a virgin in front of four obvious skanks. "You don't have to tell me if you don't want to."

Rebecca blinked her eyes drunkenly in an effort to compose herself. "Actually, we all are. See, we made this pact." She glanced around the table at her friends. "Georgetown doesn't have sororities, but we sort of have one. We call it the sisterhood of celibacy."

Blair's eyes opened wide. She was about to get indoctrinated into some sort of virginity cult, and she was so drunk and upset and vulnerable, it actually sounded like a good idea.

"We aren't, like, against fooling around or anything. God no. All of us have done just about everything *but* go all the way," Gaynor clarified. She rubbed her pug nose. "We're saving that for marriage."

"Or at least true love," Fran clarified. "I'm *never* getting married."

"Fran's parents have each been married and divorced three times," Rebecca noted.

Blair stamped out her cigarette. Fuck Nate. Fuck Yale. All of a sudden she wanted nothing more than to pledge their little sorority. "Me too," she admitted. "I mean, I'm a virgin, too."

The four girls stared at her in amazement, as if they couldn't quite believe that a sophisticated New York girl like herself had never once experienced sex.

"You totally have to join," Fran said in her hoarse, intense whisper. "And when you go here, we'll all be together. Not just until graduation, but forever!"

Blair put her elbows on the table and leaned forward, ready for action. "What do I have to do?"

The four girls giggled giddily, like they just *loved* their initiation rites.

"I'm the newest member," Forest explained.

"Her hair was almost black before," Gaynor put in.

"First you have to let us shave your legs," Fran said.

"And then we bleach your hair," Rebecca added.

And they had a problem with the whole jizz-on-a-cracker thing?!

Blair sat back in her chair. Her life was shit, and besides, she'd always wanted to know what she'd look like as a blond. She picked up her drink and poured it down her throat, banging the glass down on the table when she was done. "I'm ready," she told her new sisters.

"Yippee!" the girls chorused, and poured themselves another round.

"If I don't eat something soon," Rebecca moaned, "I'm gonna hurl."

"Me too," the other girls agreed.

"We gotta get to the drug store before it closes," Rebecca added. "We can pick up some Combos or something."

Yummy. Maybe they could even have fried pork rinds!

Blair grabbed her purse and rose shakily to her feet. "Last one in the cab is a drunk virgin bitch."

The five girls linked arms and staggered out into the night.

Question: Even if they were your new best friends, would you let four drunk virgin bitches shave your legs and dye your hair?

two's company, three's a crowd

"This is awesome," Dan enthused as he watched the spaghetti boiling in its pot. He glanced at Vanessa, who was standing next to him, slicing onions on a chopping board balanced over the sink. Onion tears streamed down her face. He kissed her damp cheek. "Look at us."

Vanessa laughed and kissed him back. Actually, this whole living-together thing *was* fun. Ruby had left early that morning, and with one taxi ride full of stuff, Dan was all moved in. They'd spent the afternoon grocery shopping and buying stupid little things for the apartment like pet rock refrigerator magnets and black sheets with neon green UFOs on them. Now they were cooking their first meal together as a cohabiting couple.

If you can call spaghetti with onions and Ragu *cooking*.

Dan slipped one hand under Vanessa's shirt and turned the burner off with the other. Dinner could wait. Their faces pressed together, they staggered out of the open kitchen area and into the living room, where they fell back onto Ruby's futon, which was now their living room couch. It still smelled like Christian Dior Poison and that licorice tea Ruby was always drinking, but it was all theirs and they could have sex on it whenever they liked.

"What will we do on Monday when we both don't want to go to school?" Vanessa wondered out loud as Dan kissed his way down her arm.

Her hands smelled like onions. "Cut? It's not like we have to worry about getting into college anymore," Dan said.

She whipped his belt out of his pants and flicked it at his butt. "Bad boy. Remember what your dad said? If your grades drop, you have to move back."

"Hey, that feels good," Dan joked.

"Oh, yeah?" Vanessa giggled, whipping him with the belt a little harder this time.

And then someone sneezed.

Dan and Vanessa broke away from each other, freaked out of their minds. A girl was standing in the doorway. Purple-and-black matted hair. Black shorts. Ripped black Ozzfest T-shirt. Black kneesocks. Black Converse high-tops. She was carrying some sort of pick-axe and an army-issue duffel bag.

"Mind if I join you?" She kicked the door closed behind her. "I'm Tiphany. Ruby mentioned I'd be staying here?"

Ruby hadn't said anything about a friend coming to stay, but then again, Ruby wasn't the most organized human being on the planet. Vanessa extracted herself from Dan. "Ruby left for Germany today." Then she realized Tiphany had let herself in. "She gave you a key?"

"I used to live here," Tiphany explained. "Your sister and I were roommates for a while." She walked in and dumped her stuff on top of the futon where they were sitting. Then she bent down and opened her duffel bag. A little head with beady eyes and whiskers popped out. Tiphany picked the creature up and cradled it like a baby.

Dan blanched. It looked like a rat.

"What is that?" Vanessa asked, intrigued. Ruby had never

mentioned anyone named Tiphany, but Ruby had lived in Williamsburg a whole year by herself before their parents had let Vanessa come down from Vermont to join her. A lot of stuff had probably happened in that year that Vanessa didn't know about.

"This is Tooter. He's a ferret. He has some farting issues, and he kind of likes to chew books. But he sleeps all curled up next to me every night, and he's such a doll." Tiphany stoked the ferret under the chin. "Aren't you, Tooter?" She held the creature out to Vanessa. "Wanna hold him?"

Vanessa reached for the scrawny animal and held it in her arms. The ferret gazed up at her with its beady brown eyes. "Isn't he cute?" she asked, and smiled over at Dan. Having houseguests made her feel like she and Dan were even more of a couple, and Tiphany seemed way cooler and more interesting than anyone she went to school with, that was for sure.

Dan didn't return her smile. Ever since he'd opened his college acceptance letters he'd been on a simple, happy high. He was into college and back with Vanessa. They were living together. Everything was easy and good. Tiphany was not part of that equation.

"What's that for?" Vanessa asked, pointing at the pick-axe.

Tiphany picked it up and swung it in the air a few times. Then she propped it up against the wall. "Work. I'm in construction. Demolition, mostly. I've got a big project over by the Brooklyn Navy Yard and I'm kind of homeless at the moment. So it was pretty cool of Ruby to let me crash here."

Vanessa turned to Dan. "The noodles," she said urgently.

Dan got up and went into the kitchen. He opened the jar of Ragu, dumped it and the onions into a saucepan, and turned the burner up to high. Then he poured the steaming pot of noodles into the colander in the sink. He pulled three bowls out of the cupboard.

"I guess anyone who wants to eat can eat," he called out.

"I'm starving. Oh, and I have a little present for us." Tiphany dug around in her duffel bag and pulled out a half-empty bottle of Jack Daniels. She poured a little Jack into the bottle cap and held it out to Tooter. "Puts hair on his chest," she told Vanessa, and took a swig from the bottle.

Vanessa handed over the ferret and went to help Dan find the silverware. "Are you okay?" she whispered.

Dan didn't answer. He spooned instant coffee into a cup and mixed it with hot water right out of the tap. Tiphany put Tooter down and the ferret scampered over to a pile of Dan's poetry books and started nibbling on them.

"No!" Dan shouted, throwing his spoon at the little rodent.

"Hey, don't yell at him!" Tiphany cried, scooping Tooter up again and holding him against her chest. "He's just a baby."

Vanessa offered her a bowl of spaghetti. "Dan's a poet," she said, as if that explained everything.

"I can see that," Tiphany said without a hint of bitterness. She took the bowl and brought it over to the futon to eat. Tooter sat in her lap, balanced his paws on the bowl's edge, and began noisily slurping up noodles.

Suddenly the entire apartment stank of rotten eggs, sour milk, and burning sulphur. Tiphany cover her mouth with her hand and snorted. "Oops! Tooter tooted!"

Talk about a buzzkill.

"Jesus." Dan grabbed a dish towel and pressed it against his nose and mouth.

"Come on," Vanessa whispered with her fingers clamped over her nose. "It's not so bad. She's *nice*."

Dan stared at her over the dish towel. He could feel himself crashing down from his high at an alarming rate and was disappointed with himself for being so annoyed by a girl who actually did seem perfectly nice, in a kooky, ferret-loving way.

He tossed aside the dish towel, served himself up some spaghetti, and carried it over to the other end of the futon. "So," he began, deciding to make an effort, "where'd you go to college?"

Tiphany giggled and wound her spaghetti around her fork. "The school of life," she answered gaily.

"Cool," Vanessa responded. "I have to interview you for my film."

"*Cool*," Dan agreed with slightly too much zeal.

Or maybe not so cool.

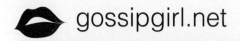
hey people!

Where do we belong?

Ever wonder what your life would have been like if you went to a different school in a different town and had a completely different set of friends? You'd probably look completely different than you do now; talk different, dress differently. You'd do different after-school activities, listen to different music. Well, that's exactly what's happening with this whole which-college-should-I-go-to? thing. Of course, your parents and teachers will tell you it doesn't matter where you go, it's what you make of it. I'm sure that's *partly* true. But if I'm not going to fit in at a certain school because everyone there wears Seven jeans instead of Blue Cults or thinks carrying your caramel poodle puppy around with you everywhere in a Burberry doggie tote is pretentious, I want to know *now*.

Not that the jeans or the dog make the girl. Well . . . actually, they sort of *do*.

The good thing about all of this is that if any of us have made or are about to make any major social-status-altering blunders, we'll have the blank canvas of college with which to reinvent ourselves. And it looks like some of us are going to be reinventing big-time. Remember that guy who didn't get in *anywhere*? His dad had the brilliant idea that military school was the place for him. Four more years of uniforms. No Prada. A crew cut. And no more monograms!

Your e-mail

Q:
Dear GG,

I go to Georgetown and I'm pretty sure I saw this girl **B** you're always talking about hanging out with all these skanks in this skanky karaoke bar where only skanks go, and she was having the time of her life. They were totally shitfaced and got driven back to campus by this greasy-looking guy in a Lexus.
—dia

A:
Dear dia,

Do I detect jealousy in your tone? What did these supposed skanks ever do to you? I think it's nice **B**'s branching out and making some new friends.
—GG

Q:
Dear GG,

I thought **N** was already into all the Ivy League schools, but then I think I saw him and the woman who interviewed me in at Brown in this restaurant where I was with my parents, and it kind of looked like they were about to hook up. What's his deal?
—celeste

A:
Dear celeste,

Good question. Maybe he's worried Brown will change their minds. Or maybe he's just sick of being denied so many times by you-know-who!
—GG

Sightings

J with a personal shopper in **Bloomingdale's**, getting more lingerie advice. At least she's finally seeking professional help—thank heavens! **N** and his **Brown** admissions officer riding up the elevator together in the **Warwick New York Hotel**. Let me guess: She wanted to conduct a second interview. **B** and four drunk blond girls in a **Georgetown** Walgreens buying disposable razors and blond hair dye. **S** lying on the roof of the art studio at Brown counting stars with some Latin-lover type. Man, that girl gets around! **D**, **V**, and some ferret-toting older girl with purple-and-black hair in a **Williamsburg** coffee shop doing espresso shots. Looks like **D** has settled in with the locals nicely.

I have a feeling it's going to be a long and sordid night—like that's so unusual. Drink lots of Red Bull and Gatorade in the morning and by Monday you'll be good as new. Can't wait to hear all about it!

You know you love me,

gossip girl

the morning after

"Guess it's a good thing I'm already into Brown, huh?" Nate said cockily. He lit the joint he'd just rolled, took a hit, and passed it to Brigid. Then he stood up and yanked on his khakis before pacing over to the window. Brigid's room at the Warwick New York Hotel looked out onto an air shaft. The room was all right, if you liked floral patterns and brown carpet, but it wasn't exactly the Plaza.

"Don't they serve coffee in the rooms in this dive?" he demanded.

Brigid was sitting up in bed, naked, with the covers draped loosely over her. "There's a restaurant downstairs, but they charge, like, five bucks for a cup of tea."

Nate whirled around. "So?" He wanted her to feel like the entire night had been a mistake. That accepting him at Brown had been a mistake.

She balanced the joint on the rim of a glass ashtray. "You know, I don't usually do this," she said, her blue-green eyes darting up and down his body as though trying to read him.

Nate opened the wooden entertainment cabinet across from the bed and flicked on the TV. He began watching a sports roundup on MSNBC, purposely ignoring her.

"I like you. You know that, right?" Brigid demanded, burning holes into his back. "We did this because we genuinely like each other?"

Nate didn't respond.

Brigid pulled the covers up to her chin. "You're not going to tell anyone at Brown about this, are you?"

He clicked off the television and tossed the remote on the bed. Brigid looked seriously worried now, which was exactly what he wanted. "Maybe," he replied. "Maybe not."

She bit her lip. Her strawberry blond hair was sticking out in all directions. "Your admission would be withdrawn," she warned.

Perfect. Nate stuck his feet into his shoes and pulled his half-unbuttoned shirt on over his head.

"And I could get fired."

He grabbed the joint from out of the ashtray and sucked on it. "I gotta run," he hissed, holding in the hit. He was due for brunch with the Yale coach in just over an hour, and he wanted to get good and buzzed first. He squeezed the joint out between his fingers and tucked it into his pocket. "Maybe we should have stuck with the lobster," he told Brigid, tucking in his shirt.

She opened her mouth and then closed it again. Her eyes were red-rimmed, as if she was about to cry. "That's it?"

"That's it," Nate said, and then he spun around and quietly took his leave.

See ya!

Out in the hallway he stabbed at the button for the elevator and waited for it with his forehead pressed against the wall. He'd never been that nasty to anyone—at least, not on purpose—and he felt horrible about it. Still, he'd done it for Blair, and it wasn't as if he'd ever follow through and get Brigid fired. All he wanted was a letter from Brown telling him they didn't want him after all.

And after that little performance, he'd probably get it.

the morning after, part ii

"Where the fuck are you, anyway?" Erik demanded.

"Shush," Serena whispered into the phone. "I'm in the art building. In a painting studio." She glanced at Christian. He was lying on the floor next to her, asleep on top of a piece of unused canvas. There was green paint in his hair. "We fell asleep in here."

"Oh, did we?" Erik responded mockingly. "I can't believe you're here and I'm not even going to see you," he whined, pretending to be hurt, when Serena knew he'd probably been up all night partying and wanted nothing more than to go back to sleep. "So, are you like in love, or what?"

Serena smiled. Christian's long-lashed brown eyes were closed and his sweet mouth was relaxed. He looked like a sleeping baby. "I'm not sure," she said softly. "I'm supposed be leaving for Yale now." She closed her eyes. "This weekend has been so crazy."

"It's not over yet, babe," Erik yawned. "I can't believe I'm even awake. It's only nine o'clock on a Sunday morning, for fuck's sake! Anyway, I'll call you a car. He'll meet you on the road right by the parking lot over there. No more picking up random boys in gas stations. Have fun at

Yale today, although you better go to Brown so we can hang. Talk to you soon. You know you love me. 'Bye!" he burbled nonsensically before hanging up.

Serena clicked off, wondering if she should wake Christian or let him sleep. A lime-juice mustache had dried on his upper lip from the Brazilian cocktails he'd made them last night, and there were little green paint flecks all over his dark olive skin. She was a little paint-smeared and rumpled herself, but Serena was the kind of girl who could sleep on the floor of an art studio all night, wake up and kick the creases out of her jeans, run her fingers through her hair, rub a little cherry-flavored ChapStick on her lips, and voilà—instagoddess.

Sunlight stalked the tall, wood-framed windows of the art studio. From where she stood, the redbrick buildings of the Brown campus looked serene and sleepy, almost like a ghost town. Then a group of students walked down the path directly in front of the window, wearing old sweatpants and carrying huge travel mugs of coffee. Serena slid away from Christian and pulled on her brown Calvin Klein flats. Leaning against the opposite wall of the studio was Christian's now-finished life-size copy of the ad for Serena's Tears. It was difficult to understand why he'd used so much green, since the ad was shot on a snowy day in February, but even with all that green, the painting was stunning. And bizarre. Christian had developed a technique in which he used only one line to complete an image. In the painting, the features in Serena's face were all connected. Her eyes connected to her nose, which connected to her mouth, which connected to her chin, her cheeks, her ears, her hair. It kind of made her look like something out of *Shrek,* especially with all that green, but it was still beautiful in its own unique way.

She retrieved a tube of Chanel lip gloss from out of her bag, found a scrap of paper on the floor, and wrote, *I like the green,* in pink sparkles. *Come see me in NYC. Love, S.* Then she pushed the piece of paper toward Christian, grabbed her bag, and tiptoed out the door.

"Au revoir," she whispered, turning to blow the sleeping boy a kiss. She hesitated. Was it sleazy to creep away without even saying good-bye? Not when they'd done nothing more than kiss and fall asleep in each other's arms. Besides, the note was pretty romantic.

A car honked noisily and Christian stirred. Serena slipped stealthily out the door and down the stairs. She'd never liked good-byes, and if Christian woke up, she'd never make it to Yale.

"Love you," she whispered as she left the building. She knew the Brown campus well enough from visiting Erik to find her way to the parking lot. Ignoring the paved walkway, she traipsed down a grassy hill, her shoes damp with dew and her pants legs covered with freshly mown grass. A black town car was pulled over at the side of the road, waiting for her, and all of a sudden she was hit with a bad case of déjà vu. Was it only yesterday that Drew had kissed her good-bye at the top of his Harvard dormitory steps, while her town car waited to whisk her up to Brown? Was it only yesterday that she'd told another boy, "I love you"?

Yup, that's right. Yesterday.

The driver opened the door for her and she got in. "I love *you* too," she whispered to Drew in apology, even though he wasn't there. A weekend away visiting schools was supposed to help clarify things, but Serena felt more confused than ever. How would she ever concentrate at college when college was full of boys just waiting for her to fall in love with them?

There's always the Dorna B. Rae College for Women in Bryn Mawr, Pennsylvania. They're still taking applications!

the morning after, part iii

"Hair of the dog, sister."

Blair opened one eye to find Rebecca standing over her, brandishing a huge Bloody Mary, complete with celery stick, lemon wedge, and pink flamingo cocktail stirrer. Rebecca's dyed blond hair was freshly blow-dried and she was wearing a pink terrycloth Juicy Couture tracksuit and electric blue eyeliner.

Hair of the dog. It was the perfect expression for how Blair felt—like a grungy, matted clump of dog hair. She tried to sit up and then fell back on the inflatable mattress again, moaning. Her scalp stung. Her legs burned. She smelled weird. What was wrong with her?

No comment.

"I swear to God you'll feel better after you drink this." Rebecca knelt down and cradled Blair's head like a mom offering her sick child some warm broth. "It's our secret recipe."

How reassuring.

Blair sat up, wincing as she gulped the thick red concoction. It tasted like vodka and barbecue potato chips.

Blech!

"Your hair will look a lot better after the roots start to grow in," Rebecca told her. "And you might want to think about bleaching your eyebrows to match."

Blair had forgotten about her hair. She knew it was blond now, or at least some semblance of blond, but she couldn't bear to look at it until she was home and within range of the Elizabeth Arden Red Door Salon. Rebecca would have to loan her a hat.

The girls' room had two sets of bunk beds, set up perpendicular to each other so the four friends could talk and giggle the night away. The beds were empty.

"Where are the others?" Blair croaked. Her mouth felt like it had been basted with nail polish.

"Getting bagels." Rebecca pulled her hair back into a tight ponytail. "Every Sunday we eat bagels and talk about the boys we could have slept with the night before but didn't."

What excellent fun.

Blair was way too hung over to discuss bagels or boys. "I have to get home," she mumbled. At home she could lie on her bed, watch old movies, and eat croissants off the tray Myrtle brought her. She could write Nate a nasty e-mail. And she wouldn't have to look at the disturbing Easter bunny mobile made of red LifeStyles condoms that the girls had hung from their dorm room ceiling.

"You can't leave until they come back," Rebecca insisted. She sat down on the bottom bunk nearest Blair, unzipped a metallic pink manicure kit, and began to clean her toenails with a pointy stainless-steel instrument. "We have to teach you our special cheer."

Blair decided right then and there that if she ever lived in a college dorm, she was definitely getting a single. No way was she sitting around with a bunch of girls while they picked at their toes or built mobiles made of condoms. She'd gone to an all-girls school since first grade—that was quite enough girl time, thank you very much.

Hauling herself to her feet, she tried to maintain her composure while wearing the light blue Powerpuff Girls nightgown Gaynor had loaned her last night. She needed a shower and then she needed to go home. Actually, fuck the shower. Showers involved bathrooms with mirrors—and seeing herself in a mirror was something she wanted to avoid at all costs.

She pulled on her jeans, wincing as they chafed against her shaved-raw legs. Then she yanked her white linen blouse on over her head, feeling way too sick to be wearing such a nice top. She hung the nightgown on the back of somebody's desk chair. "I have to go *now*," she insisted. A gray Georgetown baseball hat lay on the floor. "Is that yours?" she asked Rebecca.

"Take it," Rebecca offered generously.

Blair snatched up the hat and put it on. "Tell everyone thank you and good-bye for me," she said weakly.

Then the dorm room door burst open and Forest, Gaynor, and Fran tumbled inside carrying paper bags full of warm, freshly baked bagels and steaming cups of hot coffee. Blair's stomach churned with a mixture of nausea and starvation.

"Oh my God, you're leaving?!" Forest cried. She dropped her bags and threw herself at Rebecca and Blair. "Come on girls, circle time!"

Blair clamped her mouth shut tight as vomit threatened to spew out from between her teeth. She'd gotten up too quickly. Or maybe she shouldn't have drunk the Bloody Mary.

Or let four drunk girls shave her legs and maim her hair.

The girls stood in a tight circle, their hands clasped. Blair swayed between Rebecca and Forest, the combined odors of their perfumes making her even more nauseated.

"What do we say . . . ?" Fran whispered with hoarse enthusiasm. It sounded like the opening line to some sort of chant.

"What do *we* say when *he* says, 'Come on, you know you want to'?" the four girls chanted. "We say, '*Wait, asshole!*'"

The girls leaned into the circle in a sort of blond headlock. "No sex without true love. Friendship now and *forever*!" They broke apart whooping and jumping up and down like cheerleaders.

"I have to go," Blair mumbled for the fiftieth time, her stomach still roiling. She stumbled for the door, hoping to make it to the bathroom in time, but it was too late. Instead, she whipped the Georgetown baseball hat off her head and upchucked into it.

"I'll call you a car." Rebecca grabbed the phone and began dialing efficiently. "We don't want you to miss your plane."

Sisterhood was nice, but nobody wanted a sick sister barfing in their bedroom.

"Here." Fran held out a blue baseball cap with a white *Y* on it. A Yale cap. "You can wear mine."

Blair took the cap with her to the bathroom. A split-second glance in the mirror made it very clear that she definitely needed a hat. And sunglasses. And a whole new life.

the morning after, part iv

"It takes him a really long time to get dressed in the morning, even though, you know, he always looks like that," Dan heard Vanessa tell Tiphany when he woke up. He was lying on his back in Vanessa's bed, listening to their voices outside the door as they clattered around the kitchen making breakfast.

Looks like *what*? he wondered.

"Hey, it takes time to master the half-untucked shirt," Tiphany responded. Then Vanessa said something that Dan couldn't hear and both girls broke into a fit of laughter.

Tiphany was poaching an egg in the microwave. Vanessa had her camera propped on her shoulder. "So tell me why you chose not to go to college," she asked.

Tiphany tied her purple-and-black hair into a knot and opened a cupboard door to get out a plate. "Actually, it wasn't really a *choice*. I just never got it together to apply.

"So what did you do when everyone else went off to school?" Vanessa prompted.

Tiphany stuck two pieces of bread in the toaster and then opened all the drawers in the kitchen, looking for a knife. "For like a year I just kicked back. Went down to Florida. Lived on the beach and gave piercings to whoever wanted one. Then I got a waitressing job on a cruise ship for a while. Then I ditched the cruise ship and stayed down in Mexico, painting houses. Then I came back and got work in construction." She grinned and licked a smear of butter off her knife. "It's been one fantastic journey."

"Wow," Vanessa remarked. Tiphany was probably the most interesting, upbeat person she'd ever met, and she could feel herself developing a crush on her. Not in a sexual way, but in a sort of I-wish-I-were-more-like-you way.

"But if you could do it all over again, would you have gone to college?" Dan called over from the bedroom doorway. He was wearing a faded red T-shirt and white boxer shorts, and his hair was wild and matted.

"Hey, sleepyhead," Tiphany replied, ignoring the question.

"Hey, sleepyhead," Vanessa said in exactly the same tone of voice. "Are you okay?"

"I'm fine." Dan tugged on his shirt uncomfortably. "Did you guys just wake up?"

"We've been up for a while," Vanessa answered vaguely.

Tiphany popped her egg out of the microwave, slid it onto her toast, and carried her plate into the living room. There was a lump under the sheet on Ruby's futon where Tooter the ferret was curled up, sleeping. Tiphany put one of her own CDs in the stereo and turned up the volume. It was something loud and harsh that Dan had never heard before. Definitely not morning music. She danced over to Vanessa and took her hands, and to Dan's amazement Vanessa started hopping around and wiggling her butt in time to the music.

Hello?

Vanessa didn't dance. Ever. What had Tiphany done to her?

While the girls continued to dance, Tooter slithered out from underneath the covers and trotted over to Dan's new blue-and-gold vintage street Pumas, which were parked by the front door. He sniffed them a few times, then turned around, squatted down, and began to pee.

"Hey!" Dan cried, dashing over to rescue his shoes.

"Tooter?" Tiphany danced over. "You're okay, baby. Come to Mommy." She squatted down and held out her arms. "Don't be scared."

Vanessa joined them, her cheeks rosy from dancing. "Oh, Dan. Did you scare him?"

"No, I didn't scare him." Dan flapped his hand angrily at the ferret. "Go to Mommy, little fucker," he added under his breath.

In his head, he'd already started a new poem. It was called "Killing Tooter."

j's big debut

"Line up, girls. In size order, please!" barked Andre, the photographer's assistant.

It was eleven o'clock on Sunday morning and Jenny had arrived at the studio over an hour ago after waking up at six and spending three hours getting ready. She'd taken a shower, blow-dried her hair, and applied her makeup—three times. The first time she looked overdone, the second time she just looked freakish, and the third time she'd sensibly decided to just let herself air dry and go without makeup, since that was the stylist's job anyway.

The shoot was in the same studio as the go-see. This time the white screen and red velvet chaise were gone, replaced by a giant piece of Astroturf covering the floor and a volleyball net set up over the Astroturf. When Jenny arrived, she discovered she wasn't the only "model" being photographed. There were five other girls, and all of them looked . . . like models. The stylist asked her to change into a royal blue Nike Lycra jog bra and matching Lycra shorts. Then she combed Jenny's hair back into a ponytail and brushed on some clear lip gloss. Jenny felt more ready for gym class than a photo shoot, but then she noticed that all the other models were dressed the same way.

"Form a line in front of the net. Hurry up, girls. This isn't rocket science," Andre complained.

Since she was usually the shortest girl in any group, Jenny stood at the end of the line in front of the volleyball net next to a flat-chested girl who was only few inches taller than she was. Then Andre came over and grabbed her arm, dragging her down to the other end of the line next to a tall girl with boobs that were almost as big as hers. He jostled some of the others girls in line.

"That'll do," the photographer called out, striding up on his stocky legs. He stroked his goatee, surveying the lineup. "Try putting your arms around each other's waists."

The girls did as they were told.

"Nah, too cheerleader. Step away from each other and put your hands on your hips. Legs wide." He held his camera up and peered through it. "Shoulders back, chins up, that's it," he instructed, snapping away.

Jenny did her best to look brave and strong and challenging, the way she thought a Nike model should look. She didn't have the musculature of a rock climber or a marathon runner, but neither did the other girls.

"What is this for, anyway?" she whispered to the girl next to her.

"Some teen magazine," the girl answered. "What kind of expression do you want us to make?" the same girl called out to the photographer.

"Doesn't matter." The photographer climbed onto a stepstool and continued to photograph them.

Jenny relaxed her challenging-Nike-model face. What did he mean it didn't matter? She closed her eyes and stuck out her lower lip in an exaggerated pout, testing him.

"Nice work, short girl!" the photographer called out.

Jenny opened her eyes, completely confused. She bared her teeth and wrinkled her nose. Then she stuck out her tongue.

"Excellent!" the photographer responded.

Jenny giggled. Actually, it was a lot more fun than trying to look alluring and pretty. At least she could show off her personality. And for the first time ever in front of a camera— in a jog bra, no less—she completely forgot about her boobs.

And that in itself was a sort of miracle.

*yale wants to see **n** in their jockstrap*

"How's it hanging, coach?" Nate drawled as he joined the Yale coach at her table at Sarabeth's a full forty-five minutes late. "Sorry I'm late. I'm still wasted from last night." He'd smoked two more joints since the one with Brigid in the hotel room. Now his eyes were mere slits, and he couldn't stop smiling.

Sarabeth's was bright and flowery and packed with brunching Upper East Side moms with babies and dads reading the Sunday papers. The whole place smelled like maple syrup.

"Have a seat." The coach pointed at the chair opposite her. Her mane of blond hair cascaded over her shoulders, and she was wearing red lipstick and a sort of silvery tank top. She looked like Jessica Simpson's long-lost older sister. "Nice hat," she added with a smile.

Nate was wearing one of the Yale baseball hats she'd given him. "I've got the jockstrap on, too," he told her, trying desperately to maintain a straight face. He was getting kind of good at acting like an asshole. He grabbed a muffin from out of the basket on the table and shoved the entire thing into his mouth. "I'm fucking starving," he added with his mouth full.

"Eat as much as you like," the coach told him generously. "I'm used to being around a team of hungry boys."

"Humphft," Nate grunted. This was going to be harder than he thought. He grabbed an entire pat of butter between his fingers and rammed it into his mouth with the muffin. "So tell me why I should want to play with those pansies, anyway."

The coach sipped her mimosa. "You're the type of guy who likes a challenge—I can tell. Otherwise you get bored. You do things you might later regret. My job is to kick your ass, and I promise you, I'll do it."

Nate swallowed the lump of butter. No wonder Yale's team was doing so well this year. He had to admit, he was impressed. Then again, convincing him to go to Yale was the coach's *mission*, the whole reason she'd come down to New York in the first place. And his mission was to get *de*admitted.

Maybe he was taking the wrong approach. He wiped his mouth and gazed into the coach's blue eyes with his irresistible green ones. "Has anyone ever told you that you're hot?" He reached for her leg underneath the table and held on.

The coach smiled her placid, confident smile. "I get that a lot, especially from the guys on my team."

All of a sudden Nate felt a hot, stabbing pain in his hand. "Fuck!" he cried, pulling it away. He cradled the hand in his lap. The Yale coach had stabbed him with her fork. He was bleeding!

"And I have to say I'm attracted to you. You're a good-looking boy. But I'll just have to satisfy myself with seeing you in that Yale jockstrap in the locker room next fall." She reached into her purse and tossed a Band-Aid at him. "Deal?"

All of a sudden Nate realized that Yale might be the place for him after all. And what if Blair wound up getting in? They could go to Yale together and live happily ever after. Maybe Serena would go there too, and all *three* of them would live happily ever after.

Unlikely story.

"Deal," he said, and signaled to the waiter with his good hand. He ordered a beer and then flashed the coach the same cocky, stoned smile that made girls swoon and his teachers give him As when he deserved Cs.

The coach ran her thumb over the tines of her fork. "I think I'm going to enjoy having you on my team," she said.

And we're *all* going to enjoy seeing him in that jockstrap.

yale sings its way into *s*'s heart

Serena's tour guide at Yale was a no-show, which wasn't really a surprise since she was nearly an hour late. "Come back at three," the woman at the admissions reception desk told her. "There's a tour going out then."

Serena stood outside the Yale visitors' center, a historic white house with black shutters, wondering what to do next.

"Do re mi fa so la ti do!" chorused a group of male voices farther down Elm Street.

"La, la, la, la!" the voices chorused once more.

Serena followed her ears down the street toward Yale's stately Battell Chapel. When she reached the chapel she discovered a group of boys standing in formation beneath the arched doorway, exercising their voices. She'd heard of the famous Whiffenpoofs, Yale's all-male a cappella singing group, but she'd never heard them sing. And she'd had no idea how adorable they all were!

Suddenly they broke into "Midnight Train to Georgia." She sat down at the bottom of the chapel steps, hoping they wouldn't mind if she stayed and listened. And *looked*—at the boyish blond tenor in the front who kept stepping forward and doing cute little cameo solos; at the muscular rugby player in the back who had the deepest baritone she'd ever heard; at the freckled geek who was just coming into his own; at the tall, pale, skinny boy with floppy dark hair who sang his solos with a wonderful English accent and was wearing the dandiest 1940s-style shoes Serena had ever seen.

She could have stood up and done her own little a cappella solo: *Yale boys, Yale boys. Yum, yum, yum!*

The boys sang a last long, sweet note, standing on tiptoe to draw it out. Then the blond tenor in the front of the group came humming and bebopping down the chapel steps in Serena's direction. When he reached her step he fell on his knees and gazed up at her.

"One, two, three . . . Beautiful girl, won't you fall in love with me?" he sang.

Serena giggled. Was he kidding?

"Beautiful girl, won't you be my family?" The rugby player picked up the song from the top of the steps.

"Beautiful girl, won't you waste the afternoon kissing me under a tree?" the entire group sang in harmony.

Serena sat on her hands, blushing furiously. She could see now why Blair wanted to go to Yale so badly!

"Today is Sunday, and on Sundays we sing instead of talk. It's a beautiful day. Won't you join me for a walk?" the blond tenor sang, taking her hand.

Serena hesitated. It was kind of cocky of him to just walk up and start serenading her. The boy seemed to notice her hesitation. "I'm Lars. I'm a sophomore," he whispered, as if worried that the rest of the group would hear him talking instead of singing. "That was just an improv song. We do them all the time."

Serena relaxed a little. Lars had magnificent aqua-colored eyes and the tiniest smattering of freckles on the bridge of his nose. He was also wearing the exact same pair of tan Camper shoes she'd bought her brother for his last birthday.

"I did miss my tour," she confessed.

"I'll give you a tour, no problem," he sang.

She gazed over his shoulder across College Street at Yale's old campus. A group of girls were playing Frisbee on New Haven green, the gabled windows of the ancient residence halls rising up around them. It was a beautiful place.

"Beautiful girl, we'll all *give you a tour,"* the Whiffenpoofs sang.

Serena giggled again and let Lars pull her to her feet. If Yale wanted her this bad, they could have her!

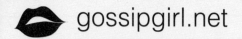 gossipgirl.net

Disclaimer: All the real names of places, people, and events have been altered or abbreviated to protect the innocent. Namely, me.

hey people!

Little-known facts (or outrageous lies—you decide)

At Georgetown there exists a prostitution ring that masks itself as a sisterhood of celibacy. It's an extremely exclusive group that's been around for half a century.

A serial killer who carries a pet ferret and uses girly exotic names for herself such as Fantasia and Tinkerbell is on the loose in the metropolitan area. Preferred weapon: the pick-axe.

A clever con artist has been disguising herself as an admissions person at Brown University, accepting students and collecting tuition. When the students show up for orientation in the fall, the university has never heard of them. So far, authorities have yet to nail down the perpetrator of this inventive scam.

The latest issue of *Treat* magazine features an article called "Does Breast Size Matter?" Are you thinking what I'm thinking?

Apparently Brown's art department has been singing the praises of its youngest professor, a Venezuelan recruit who specializes in abstract oil renditions of pop-culture figures, especially teen pop-culture figures. Again, are you thinking what I'm thinking?

Of course, this could all be a bunch of hooey.

Your e-mail

 Dear GG,
How come you're not stressing about which college to go to?

I'm beginning to think maybe you're really like in eighth grade and maybe you just have an older sister or brother or something and that's how you know about this stuff.
—bird

A: Dear bird,
I love how much time everyone spends thinking about ME. Am I going to be one of those pop icons people start writing Ph.D. papers on, like Madonna? I'll tell you this, though: Eighth grade? Been there, done that.
—GG

Q: Dear GG,
I got kicked out of Brown before I even started my freshman year. I was really surprised I was accepted there in the first place, since I got Ds in almost everything my senior year of high school. Anyway, it turns out I didn't really get in. I was part of this whole scam where somebody was accepting kids and taking their parents' money without the school even knowing. Now I'm a caddy at my dad's golf club.
—putter

A: Dear putter,
I'm kind of hoping you're just this bored stoner caddy guy, like the ones at MY dad's golf club, who likes to tell everyone this story about how he got accepted at Brown and then expelled. It's a good story. I just hope the same thing doesn't happen to me or any of my friends.
—GG

Q: Dear GG,
can u please explain the difference between a girl who just likes hanging out with different guys and a hoochie? cuz i know I may seem like a hoochie but what is so wrong with having lots of friends who are boys? none of the boys seem to mind. only the girls.
—popgrl

A: Dear popgrl,
Nothing. Nothing. Nothing. In fact, a girl very close to my heart—known here as **S**—is just that type of girl, and look how well she's doing!
—GG

Sightings

V and **D** getting dragged around **Chinatown** by a loud girl with purple-and-black hair carrying a live fish in a blue plastic bag. Let's just say I won't be dining at their house anytime soon. **B** in the **Elizabeth Arden Red Door Salon** after closing time on Sunday. Can you spell *color correction*? **S** with her head plastered against the window of the New Haven–New York train, snoring softly. Guess she didn't get much sleep this weekend—nudge, nudge. **N** on a shady street corner trading his **Brown** sweatshirt for a dime bag. And little **J** jogging in **Riverside Park**. Trying to tone up for her next modeling gig?

Who knew this would be such a life-changing weekend?

See you at school tomorrow.

You know you love me,

gossip girl

b deserves a purple heart

"Mrs. M got a call from Georgetown," Rain Hoffstetter whispered to Kati Farkas in the Constance Billard School library as the girls pretended to select books on modern American painting to read during study hall. "Saturday night Blair and a bunch of Georgetown girls were caught getting paid for sex. They went to some singles bar in town and picked up guys all night. Her mom is coming for a conference in Mrs. M's office because now she can't even go to Georgetown."

Sure enough, Blair had just told the librarian that she was skipping study hall for an important meeting in the headmistress's office *with her mother.*

"I thought she looked funny today," mused Isabel Coates. "I guess if you're going to wait this long to lose your virginity, you may as well get paid for it."

"But how come she's wearing tights? It's like seventy degrees today!" Kati pointed out.

Laura Salmon giggled. "Maybe she's got, like, rug burn—you know, from all the sex."

Or maybe she let four drunk girls shave her legs?

Mrs. M's office was on the main floor, down the hall

from the reception area. As she walked by, Blair noticed that the reception desk was covered with bouquets of flowers—roses, mostly.

"What are those for?" Blair asked Donna, the new part-time receptionist.

Donna shrugged and stamped another letter with Mrs. M's signature. "You tell me."

Blair checked the tag on the biggest bouquet, a gorgeous mix of yellow roses and freesias. *Serena, Serena,* it read. *I can't stop singing your name.* And it was signed, *Love, Lars and the Yale Whiffenpoofs.*

"It figures," Blair sulked as she headed into Mrs. M's office. Maybe if she'd been slutty enough to sleep with every guy in the Whiffenpoofs, she would have gotten into Yale, too.

Mrs. M's office was completely red, white, and blue. China-blue-and-white-striped wallpaper. Red carpeting. Navy blue velvet sofa. Red-and-white-chintz chair. It was very patriotic. Even Mrs. M was red, white, and blue—navy blue linen old-lady pantsuit, red lipstick, pasty white skin, red polished fingernails. Only her hair, which was curly and brown, varied from the color scheme.

"I do like your hair short," Mrs. M commented when Blair walked in.

Of course you do, you lesbo dyke, Blair thought, smiling politely. She patted her head. "Thank you."

Actually, she was kind of relieved that she'd made it this far into the day without anyone—even her mother—noticing that her hair had been dyed from natural dark brown to taxicab yellow and then back to brown again. The colorist had done a decent job, but to her the color was unnaturally *uniform,* and her scalp itched like crazy from all the dye.

Blair sat down on the sofa and then her mother waddled into Mrs. M's office, clutching her stomach like the baby was going to fall out if she didn't hold on to it. Pieces of her blond bob were plastered to her cheeks, and her skin was red and blotchy. She fanned herself with her hand. "This time last year I was playing a full game of tennis five days a week. Now I can't walk down the block without breaking a sweat!"

Mrs. M smiled her polite, talking-to-a-parent smile. "Running after a baby will get you back in shape in no time."

Right, as if there wasn't already a baby-nurse sleeping in the maid's room of the penthouse!

Blair rolled her eyes and scratched her razor-burned calves. She hadn't called this meeting to talk about babies. Through Mrs. M's office window she spied a woman in military fatigues walking down Ninety-third Street. The sight gave Blair an idea. Wasn't there some kind of army program that sponsored your years at college? She could join the army, go to Yale, and then do the minimum required service. She imagined herself up to her waist in the muddy trenches, fighting off the enemy, while everyone else was studying in the library or something. She could be a hero, win a Purple Heart! And when she went MIA, Nate would go after her, risking his life to get her back and finally have sex after all these years.

Saving Private Blair. Coming soon to your local video store.

Mrs. M nestled her wide, manly ass into the red toile wingback chair behind her huge mahogany desk. "While I've got you both here, I'd like to congratulate Blair on her performance at Constance. Never a grade below a B.

Excellent attendance. Wonderful show of leadership and participation. Blair, you can expect to receive a handful of awards at graduation in June."

Blair's mom smiled vaguely at the headmistress. Her mind seemed to be on other things.

"Then why didn't I get into Yale?" Blair demanded. "What's the point of working so hard and everything if a school like Yale goes and accepts some of my classmates who are way dumber than I am?"

Mrs. M sorted through the papers on her desk. "I can't speak for Yale, and I can't say I understand their decision. But our records show you were wait-listed. There's still a very good chance you'll get in."

Blair crossed her arms over her chest. That wasn't good enough. She glared at her mom. Now was when her mom was supposed ply Mrs. M with lots of money for Constance if Mrs. M put in a few calls to Yale's dean of admissions and secured Blair a place. But Eleanor just sat there staring out the window and panting through her mouth like a dog in summer.

"Mom?" Blair demanded.

"Whoosh," Eleanor panted, fanning herself frantically. "Would you mind calling me a car, dear?" She pried herself out of her chair and squatted on Mrs. M's crimson carpet in a pose Blair recognized from Ruth's birth class. "Whoooosh! I think I may be further along than everyone thought!"

Talk about timing.

Blair grimaced as her mother went into serious birth-class-breathing-exercise mode.

"Whoosh, whoosh, whoosh!"

"Mom!"

Mrs. M dialed Donna in reception. "Call an ambulance,

please, Donna. Mrs. Waldorf Rose appears to be in labor."

"No!" Blair countered. "Lenox Hill isn't far. Mom's car is waiting for her out front." Her mother grabbed her hand and squeezed it hard. Blair had the feeling she'd said the right thing.

"Scratch that," Mrs. M commanded in that military commando voice the girls always made fun of. "Mrs. Rose's car is waiting outside the school. Please tell her driver she's coming out and needs to get to Lenox Hill Hospital."

"Whoosh, whoosh, whoosh!" Eleanor panted.

"Now," Mrs. M barked into the phone.

Blair extracted her phone from her bag and called Cyrus. "Mom's in labor," she told his voicemail flatly. "We're going to the hospital." She clicked off and tucked her hands under her mom's armpits. "You don't want to have her here, Mom, do you?"

"No," Eleanor whimpered, and staggered to her feet. She wrapped one arm around Blair's shoulder and the other around Mrs. M's waist. "Whoosh, whoosh, whoosh," she panted as the odd threesome made their way down the hall and out Constance Billard's great blue doors.

"I'll call the hospital and tell them you're coming," Mrs. M told Blair competently.

"Heart attack?" the driver asked as he opened the car door for them. He almost looked happy about it.

"No, idiot," Blair snapped. "She's having a baby. And if you'd shut up, we'd be there already."

"Whoosh, whoosh, whooee!" Her mother panted, grabbing Blair's hand in a death grip.

Blair looked up at Constance's tall third-floor library windows as the car pulled away from the curb. The windows were crowded with the faces of girls peering down at the street.

"Oh my God. I think she just had her baby in Mrs. M's office!" Rain Hoffstetter cried.

"Who? Blair?" asked Laura Salmon.

"No, stupid. Her *mom*," Rain corrected.

"It's totally Blair's fault. I heard stress can cause you to go into labor early," Isabel Coates observed.

"Her poor mom. It's like, oh, by the way, your daughter is a prostitute. And oops, here comes another kid for you to fuck up!" Nicki Button added.

"Baby's coming! Wheeesh!" Eleanor hissed, getting on all fours in the back of the town car. "Baby's coming *now*," she growled, biting the vinyl headrest.

Blair turned away from the window and reached up to pat her mother's shoulder. "We're almost there, Mom," she murmured, glad that she'd been around when her mom went into labor, instead of some annoying salesperson in Saks or something. "Just imagine you're . . ." She tried to think of something Ruth had told them in class, but the only thing she could remember was the buttocks-deflating-like-a-balloon thing, and no way was she saying *that*. Instead she tried to think of what made *her* relax. "Just imagine you're eating a big bowl of chocolate ice cream and watching *Breakfast at Tiffany's*," she said finally.

"Baby's coming *now*!" her mother shrieked again, her knuckles white and her face purple with effort.

Blair realized it didn't much matter what she said. The baby *was* coming—it was only a matter of minutes. The car stopped at a light at Eighty-ninth and Park. She scooted forward and leaned close to the driver's ear. "Do you want us to completely fuck up the backseat of your car, or are you going to run this light and get us there in the next thirty seconds?"

The driver stepped on the gas, pressing down hard on his horn at the same time.

Baby's coming!

n and *s* miss their old threesome

Nate was on his way out of school to pick up a burrito and a dime bag for lunch when he stopped short. A woman with strawberry blond hair was seated on the brown leather bench just inside the school doors, her black Kate Spade pocketbook perched neatly on her knees and a Brown University duffel bag at her feet. A fat novel lay open in her lap, and it looked like she'd been there for hours. Nate crept backwards down the stairs to the basement locker area. This time he would have to ignore the munchies and forgo his usual pretrig joint. Either that or risk facing Brigid.

"Dude, what're you sneaking around for?" Jeremy asked, watching him from the foot of the stairs.

"No reason," Nate grumbled. "Hey, you eaten yet?" he asked hopefully.

"Nah. I'm headed to the deli right now. Wanna come?" Jeremy patted his baggy khaki pants pocket so Nate could hear the dry crinkle of rolling papers and a bag full of weed. "Have a little appetizer first?"

Nate pulled a twenty-dollar bill out of his pocket and handed it to his friend. "Just get me a tuna sandwich and a Gatorade or something."

Jeremy took the money. "What, didn't finish your trig homework again?"

"Didn't even start it yet."

Jeremy swung his backpack around and pulled a notebook out of it. He handed it to Nate. "Start copying. I'll bring your food down when I get back."

"Thanks, man," Nate said gratefully. The truth was, Jeremy sucked even worse at trig than he did, but he was still world-class as far as friends went.

"Hey," Jeremy called, stopping at the top of the stairs. "Did you hear about Blair's mom? Guess she had her baby, like, in a meeting at Blair's school."

Nate stared at his friend, too scared to reply for fear Brigid would hear. He raised his hand and nodded stiffly before stalking into the crowded locker area. Jesus fucking Christ. Could Blair's life get any more melo-fucking-dramatic?

Stick around and find out.

The downstairs locker area was the only place in school where you could use "handheld devices." Boys milled around listening to their MP3 players or huddled in groups watching a DVD on someone's laptop. Nate sat down on the cold, vomit-green linoleum floor in front of his locker, whipped out his phone, and buzzed Serena on her cell. Of course he couldn't call Blair. Not when she was at the hospital attending to her mom and everything.

As if he'd call her anyway. Scaredy-cat.

Serena sat in a coveted window seat in the Constance Billard library, pretending to ignore the gossip flying around the room, especially since half of it was about her. She was perfectly aware of the fact that the school reception area downstairs looked like an exhibit at Macy's flower show, and that all the flowers were from her Ivy League admirers. But how could she enjoy being in love with three different guys when she had no one with whom to share the excitement? And how was she supposed to pick one boy without some objective advice from her best friend?

Wait, isn't she supposed to be picking a *school*?

Obviously Blair was pissed as hell at her over the whole Yale thing and wasn't about to talk to her. Plus it looked like Blair was going to be kind of preoccupied for a while anyway, what with her baby sister arriving so unexpectedly. And it wasn't as if Serena could go up to one of her supposed friends and classmates like Isabel Coates or Kati Farkas, because, based on the loudly whispered rumors circulating at school, it was generally thought that Serena had had sex with the entire orchestra at Harvard, every professor in Brown's art department, and every Whiffenpoof at Yale.

"I heard she even did it with the first-chair violinist," one girl murmured indiscreetly. "He's like this fifteen-year-old prodigy from Japan."

"You know the art professor she hooked up with at Brown? He's like the oldest teacher there. He's been there since the school was *founded*."

Since 1764? Wow, he *is* old!

"I heard she stole the Audrey Hepburn screenplay Blair wrote for Yale. That's how she got in. Blair found out and now they're, like, total enemies again."

Being the subject of such outrageous tales was nothing new to Serena. Her mysterious return to Constance that fall after almost two years away at boarding school had turned her into a veteran of half-truths and petty gossip. She knew the best way to handle it, too: ignore it.

All of a sudden her cell phone buzzed and vibrated in her pink canvas Lulu Guinness rucksack. She took a peek and recognized Nate's number. "Hey," she whispered, holding the phone to her ear, behind her giant chemistry textbook. "Did you hear about Blair's mom?"

"That's why I'm calling," Nate replied. "What happened?"

Serena wasn't the type to tell tall tales. "I'm not sure. All I really know is Blair went to a meeting with the headmistress and her mom, and then all of a sudden she and her mom were, like, running into a car outside school. The receptionist told some girls in our class she was in labor and the car was headed for Lenox Hill."

"Jesus," Nate muttered.

"I know," Serena responded. "She wasn't supposed to have it until June."

"Do you think we should go to the hospital? Like maybe tomorrow or something? We could bring flowers and—"

"I don't know," she answered doubtfully, although she certainly had a lot of flowers to recycle. "It's kind of a private family thing. We may not be welcome."

Actually, Blair's mom had always treated them like family. Blair was the one who wouldn't welcome them, and they both knew it.

"Yeah," Nate agreed. "You're probably right. I guess I just . . ." His voice drifted off.

"I know," Serena said softly.

They both wished they were a threesome all over again, there for one another in times like this. Too bad Blair was mad as fuck at them.

"The crazy thing is, I'm kind of leaning toward going to Yale," Nate admitted. "Blair's going to kill me."

Serena stared out the window. A dog walker led twenty

dogs at once down the street toward Central Park, his head tilted back, singing at the top of his lungs.

"I'm kind of leaning toward Yale, too," she said, even though she wasn't completely convinced. Drew, Christian, or Lars? How would she ever decide? "Or maybe I should just take a year off."

"We could all wind up at Yale together," Nate mused.

Now *that* would be something.

"Maybe," Serena agreed. The library felt incredibly *still* all of a sudden. She peeked over her textbook to see what was up, and forty pairs of eyes glanced quickly away. The entire room had been eavesdropping on her conversation.

Well, it served her right for talking on the phone in the library, which we all know is against school policy.

"I better go," she told Nate quickly. "Bell's gonna ring any minute."

"Hey," Nate said before she could hang up, "is that girl with the shaved head still interviewing people in the park?"

"I think so," Serena replied.

"Cool," he answered, sounding distracted. "Later," he added, before clicking off.

Serena popped her textbook closed. Maybe she could press some of the flowers she'd been sent inside that very book and use them to make Blair's mom a cute card or something.

Nate tucked his phone back into his pocket and shot upstairs from the locker area, on his way to the local florist to send Blair's mom some flowers. Just in time, he remembered why he'd been hunkered down in the locker area in the first place. Brigid was still camped out up there, waiting for him.

He swung around and walked slowly back downstairs again as he dialed 411. Blair had always talked about how

when they had an apartment together she would order flowers from Takashimaya three times a week. She was pretty
fussy about flowers. He got the number and punched it in.

"I'd like to send flowers to a patient at Lenox Hill Hospital
in Manhattan," Nate told the woman on the other line.

Jeremy tripped down the stairs behind him. "Nice," he noted,
handing Nate a brown paper bag and a handful of change.

"Just put, 'Love, comma, Nate,' on the card," Nate instructed.
Nice.

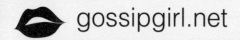
Disclaimer: All the real names of places, people, and events have been altered or abbreviated to protect the innocent. Namely, me.

hey people!

NY Times birth announcement

I did their wedding announcement, and now it's only . . . ahem, five months later, and I'm doing the birth announcement. Here goes:

Yale Jemimah Doris Rose, daughter. Due in early June, the little munchkin just couldn't wait. Instead, she decided to be born at Lenox Hill Hospital on the Upper East Side of Manhattan at 2:17 P.M., April 20—yesterday. Total labor time: forty-five minutes. Weight: eight pounds, nine ounces. Height: nineteen inches. If she'd waited any longer, she'd have been a Big Mac instead of just a Whopper Jr. The glowing parents are Eleanor Wheaton Waldorf Rose, society hostess, and Cyrus Solomon Rose, real estate developer, of East Seventy-second Street. Siblings are Aaron Elihue Rose, 17; Tyler Hugh Waldorf Rose, 12; and Blair Cornelia Waldorf, 17, who is responsible for the baby's unusual first name. Blair is obviously hoping her new baby sister will bring her luck at the university of the same name—heaven knows she could use some. Mother and child are doing fine, and the happy family will be returning to their penthouse tomorrow afternoon.

Your e-mail

 Dear GG,

Last night I found my older brother reading my *Treat* magazine in bed. I got it back from him, but he showed me the page he was all into. It's this girl in my class at Constance in a jog bra that's way too small for her standing there with all these other models, like in boob-size order. My brother asked if he could rip

it out and put it in his locker. I told him no, but I think he's going to buy the magazine and do it anyway. If I was that girl, I'd die.
—phoenix

 Dear phoenix,
Let's hope for your classmate's sake that your brother doesn't have a lot of friends.
—GG

Sightings

A whole group of **Constance Billard** seniors in the **Wicker Garden** on **Madison Avenue**, cooing over baby gifts. Any excuse to shop. **J** and **E** accidentally getting on the same crosstown bus and ignoring each other the whole ride. Still mad, huh? **V** getting purple highlights at a **Williamsburg** hair salon. Wait, how can she get highlights when she has no *hair*?! **N** creeping out of the **St. Jude's School for Boys** after even the janitor had left. Boy, is he paranoid. **B** in **Zitomer** on Madison buying diapers and a three-hundred-dollar cashmere baby romper. Guess who's going to be that little girl's favorite big sister? **S** walking through the park, giving flowers away to the homeless. It's the thought that counts.

I'm off to the local newsstand to check out that mag!

You know you love me,

gossip girl

size matters

Dan walked into first-period English on Tuesday to find every guy in his class poring over some teen girl magazine.

"What people don't realize is they look even bigger in person," Chuck Bass, Dan's least favorite person at Riverside Prep and perhaps the world, observed from his usual place in the back of the classroom. Chuck was wearing the army green military-style beret he'd picked up at West Point that weekend. It was his favorite new accessory besides his pet snow monkey, which he carried with him everywhere, even to the bathroom. Chuck looked up. "Am I right?"

Dan had the uneasy feeling that Chuck was talking to him.

"It's like they're full of helium or something," another boy added, leaning over Chuck's desk to see.

Chuck shook his head. His dark hair had grown into a sort of chin-length man-bob that he swished around with obvious pride. "Dude, if they were full of helium, she'd fucking float away." He squinted down at the magazine again, his gold monogrammed pinky ring glowing beneath the harsh classroom lights. Then he looked up at Dan again. "Dude, she's your sister. What's her fucking deal?"

Dan's instinct was to tell Chuck to go fuck himself, but

since it involved his little sister, Jenny, who often blundered into all kinds of trouble, he felt he ought to check it out for himself. He sat down on the desk in front of Chuck's and put his feet up on the chair. On the floor, something wriggled inside Chuck's orange Prada messenger bag. Suddenly a white head with eyes like golden marbles popped out. It was Chuck's monkey, grinning devilishly.

Dan glared at Chuck. "What about my sister?"

Chuck smirked and handed over the magazine. "Don't tell me you don't know about this."

The magazine was open to a two-page spread entitled "Does Breast Size Matter?" The article was an earnest discussion of girls' social status based on breast size. Apparently if you were flat-chested or supersized, you were more likely to be ostracized. If you were buxom but not hideously so, you were a slut. Popular girls tended to have nice, medium-sized 34Bs. Dan studied the picture. Jenny and five other girls wearing matching blue jog bras and Lycra shorts were lined up in breast-size order, biggest to smallest, in front of a volleyball net. The other girls were all models—blond, with cheesily perfect smiles, flat tummies, and golden tans. The girl next to Jenny definitely had implants, but her chest still wasn't as big as Jenny's one hundred percent naturals. Jenny's chest looked abnormal and almost freakish, stuffed inside a jog bra that was way too small. Worse still, she was sticking out her tongue and her big brown eyes were shining, like she was having the time of her life.

"Christ," Dan muttered, and tossed the magazine back on Chuck's desk, his hands beginning to sweat and shake as they always did when he needed a cigarette. He knew the article was intended to empower girls with big chests. There was Jenny, looking freakish but proud of it. But that wouldn't stop every guy who saw the picture from ripping it out and writing some lewd comment underneath it before pasting it on the door of a bathroom stall.

"Says here eight out of ten guys prefer a gorgeous girl with average-size breasts over an average girl with supersize tits," Chuck elaborated.

Thanks, Captain Asshole, sir.

It was pretty obvious to Dan that his sister was so eager to be a model, she hadn't thought about what the picture would actually look like. Still, not long ago, a very compromising picture of Jenny had been posted all over the Internet. People had talked about it for a day or two, and then it had gone away. And Jenny had never even seemed that bothered by it. She was like Mr. Magoo, running blindly into the most embarrassing, awkward situations, and then walking out of them, unscathed and blaming nobody. Hopefully this would be the same, but just in case, Dan felt obliged to warn her.

Jenny sat by herself near the mirrored wall in the back of the Constance Billard basement cafeteria, eating a grilled cheese sandwich with pickle slices. She concentrated on neatly lining the pickles up on top of the toasted bread, trying to pretend that she didn't mind eating alone. There was a strange stillness in the air that she couldn't quite explain, but every time she glanced up at the mirrors, all she saw were the heads of the other upper-school girls, bowed over their plates, eating quietly.

Right. Since when did upper-school girls ever eat quietly? As a matter of fact, the room was *buzzing,* buzzing with the sound of that morning's juiciest scoop.

"I heard she didn't even get paid to do it—she *volunteered,*" Vicky Reinerson whispered.

"But Serena put her up to it, remember? In peer group?"

Mary Goldberg hissed. "She was like, 'Oh, Jenny, *anyone* can be a supermodel.'"

"Easy for her to say," Cassie Inwirth agreed. "But it's not like I feel sorry for Jenny. It's so obvious she just wants attention."

"Yeah, but nobody wants *that* kind of attention," Vicky countered.

The three girls stole a glance at the back of Jenny's head. How could she just sit there eating her lunch like nothing was wrong?

Jenny's cell phone rang quietly inside her bag. "Hey," she answered without even checking who'd called. Dan and Elise were the only ones who ever did anyway, and she and Elise were no longer friends. She tucked the phone under her curly brown bob to hide it from the lunch ladies. "What's up?"

"I'm just calling to check that you're okay," Dan mumbled back.

Jenny stared at her reflection in the mirror. She'd worn pink metal barrettes in her hair today, and she thought she looked sort of retro and cool. "Um, I think so."

"So no one's, like, said anything to you or . . . ," Dan faltered.

"About what? Why, did you do something weird, Dan?" Jenny accused.

"About the photo of you in that magazine? The guys here all stole it from their sisters. They're putting it up in their lockers and stuff."

A little shiver shot up Jenny's spine. Dan wouldn't be so concerned if the picture was as good as she thought it was. "Did you see it? What's wrong with it?"

He didn't respond.

"Dan!" Jenny practically shouted. "What's wrong with it?"

"It's just . . . ," Dan fumbled. "Okay, the whole thing is about how girls with no chest or really big chests aren't popular. I guess the article is supposed make you feel better, but you kind of look like a . . . circus freak next to the other girls. I mean, they basically made you look as big and freakish as possible."

Jenny slid the tray of food away and rested her head on the cold wooden table. No wonder the room seemed so quiet. Everyone had been busy whispering about her, the big-boobed freak.

Yup.

It was even worse than a Stayfree ad. She was the circus freak. Maybe she should just run away and live with her neurotic mom in Europe or something. Change her name. Dye her hair orange.

"Jenny?" Dan said gently. "I'm sorry."

"Never mind," Jenny said miserably, and clicked off. She kept her head on the table, wishing she could just disappear.

All of a sudden she felt a warm body next to hers and smelled Serena's trademark signature essential-oil mixture.

"Hey sleepyhead. So, Jonathan Joyce—you know who he is, right?—calls me, like, all excited about your Polaroids. He knows we're pals and totally wants to shoot us together, like, later this week!"

Was this some sort of vicious joke? Jenny squeezed her eyes shut as tight as they could go and tried to will Serena away.

"You'll get to keep some of the clothes," Serena added.

Jenny raised her head and stood up shakily. "Leave me alone," she murmured, then bolted out of the cafeteria to the nurse's office, where she planned to beg to be sent home.

d's little furry friends

"Tooter, look at that!" Tiphany put the ferret on her shoulder and waved his paw up and down at Chuck Bass's little white monkey. The monkey was wearing a tiny red T-shirt with the letter *S* monogrammed on it. "Hey little monkey, wanna be my friend?"

Vanessa and Tiphany had come to pick Dan up from school. "Maybe not," Vanessa warned, knowing how much Dan hated Chuck's guts.

"Hey cutie, what's your name?" Chuck came over and scratched Tooter under the chin. He held his monkey up so the two animals were nose-to-nose. "I'm Sweetie. And don't worry, I don't bite. I really am sweet."

"I'm Tooter," Tiphany chirped in her version of a ferret voice. "And beware, I really can toot!" she added, cackling hilariously.

Dan pushed open the school doors and paused at the top of the steps. He hitched his black messenger bag onto his shoulder, squinting in the harsh April sunlight. All afternoon he'd been worrying about his little sister. Jenny was probably at home right now, facedown on her bed, all alone. His house was only twenty blocks away; maybe he ought to go up there and try to cheer her up. Then again, when Jenny was upset, all she wanted was to be alone, same as him. It ran in the family.

"Hey hot stuff, over here!" Tiphany shouted at him in her glass-shatteringly loud voice. Down on the sidewalk stood Vanessa, Tiphany, and Chuck Bass. Tiphany's ferret and Chuck's monkey were perched on their owners' shoulders, grooming each other.

"Christ," Dan muttered. Maybe Chuck would move in with them, too, and they could all be one big, happy family. Or maybe he'd just tell Vanessa right now that he was going to stay at home for a while. His sister needed him.

"May we escort you home?" Vanessa stepped away from the group as Dan came down the stairs with a sour expression on his face. She kissed him quickly on the cheek. "Hey pumpkin, don't look so pissed off all the time." Dan had been acting pissed off and withdrawn ever since they'd moved in together and Tiphany had turned up. It was getting a little tiring always having to be the upbeat one in the relationship.

Pumpkin? In only a matter of days Vanessa had picked up Tiphany's over-the-top, cheery way of talking, annoying Dan even more. "I'm not pissed off," he grumbled, glaring at Chuck and Tiphany, who were bonding over their pets. "I'm just—"

Tiphany pointed her index fingers at him, like twin pistols, and pretended to shoot. "You know, Danny boy, I think what your little sister did was totally rad. Baring your tits is the boldest feminist statement a gal can make!" She'd braided the front of her hair and left the back in a sort of crazy purple-and-black rat's nest, which she probably thought was some big feminist statement, too.

Vanessa had tried not to look a moment ago when Chuck showed Tiphany the picture of Jenny, but she couldn't help herself. And the funny thing was, she actually agreed with Tiphany. Jenny may not have looked like a model, but she definitely looked *bold*.

"I think so, too," she agreed before she saw the look on Dan's face.

"She didn't bare anything," Dan told them angrily. "Jesus, she's only fourteen."

"Hey, that reminds me," Vanessa said, eager to change the subject. "In case you forgot, it's my birthday this weekend. I'm gonna be eighteen!"

Dan frowned. He and Vanessa had never made a big deal out of their birthdays before.

"And I was thinking, now that we're living together, we could have a party!" Vanessa continued.

Dan noticed there was a sort of purple glow to her hair that he hadn't seen before. "A party?" Vanessa had always hated parties. This definitely had to be Tiphany's idea.

"It's gonna be rad!" Tiphany shouted. She grabbed Tooter's paw and pointed it at Chuck's monkey. "You're coming, right?" she asked in her stupid ferret voice.

"Most definitely," Chuck chattered like a monkey.

Fucking hell.

"Come on." Vanessa pulled Dan toward Broadway. It was another sunny day and a steady stream of boys were making their way west toward the park. "First I want to do a few more interviews. Then we can go home and send e-vites."

"But—"

"Don't worry about your sister," Vanessa countered, reading his mind. "She's more together than you think." She kissed him, trying to bring a smile to his sullen lips. "Our first real party!"

Dan let her pull him away, following along with leaden

feet. He hated parties, and besides, they had no other friends. In total the guest list would consist of Chuck, Tiphany, Chuck's monkey, Tooter, and Dan's social pariah of a sister, Jenny. Some party.

Vanessa poked him in the ribs. "Come on, smile. You know you want to."

"If you don't smile, I'm going to flash my tits at you," Tiphany threatened, skipping along the sidewalk beside them in her purple-and-black-plaid John Fluevog boots. She unzipped the camouflage-print army jacket she'd borrowed from Ruby's closet and tucked Tooter into her black tank top.

"Can I flash mine, too?" Chuck joined in. His monkey had wrapped its long, snowy white tail twice around his neck. Wearing his West Point military beret, he and Tiphany sort of matched.

Dan gritted his teeth and smiled weakly just to shut them up.

"He smiled!" Vanessa and Tiphany shouted gleefully, and slapped each other five.

Here's what Dan was really thinking as he continued to smile: Evergreen College was way across the continent in the Pacific Northwest, where it rained a lot and people were depressed. He'd never seriously considered going there, but it was beginning to seem like paradise.

n bares his . . . soul

Central Park was the usual sunny afternoon mob scene of Rollerbladers, skateboarders, Frisbee throwers, and girls in bikini tops pretending they were on the beach in St. Tropez.

Vanessa set up her camera in her usual spot by Bethesda Fountain. Tiphany pulled Tooter out of her shirt and began to bathe him in the water. Dan hung back and bought one of those huge imitation ice cream cones from a vendor on the promenade. Then he sat down on a park bench to wait for Vanessa, praying Tiphany would leave him be.

"So I think I might be happy up at West Point," Chuck confided to Vanessa's camera. "As long as I can find some-one to keep Sweetie nearby so I can visit her. And they don't make me shave my head—no offense. And I get a big-ger bed than those dinky cots they make those poor losers sleep on."

Looks like he's in for a rude awakening.

"Mom promised to set me up an account at Balducci's so they'll send me a box with brie and caviar and chocolate and cigars once a week," he added. "I'll miss my apartment, but it's better than nothing. . . ." His voice trailed off, and he stuck his face into the ruff of white fur on Sweetie's neck. "West Point," he said, his voice muffled. "West fucking Point!"

All of a sudden Nate Archibald appeared beside him and Chuck looked up, grinning his obnoxious grin, like he hadn't almost just burst into tears. "I'm done if you want to go next," he said, clearly unwilling to bare his soul in front of another guy. He stood up and carried his monkey over to where Tiphany was bathing Tooter. "Can I help?" he twittered in his monkey voice.

Nate shoved his hands in his khaki pants pockets and shifted from foot to foot. Then he sat down in Chuck's place.

"I guess I really screwed up," he admitted to the camera. "I mean, my girlfriend's life is, like, a train wreck and I can't even call her." His green eyes looked sad as he watched Tiphany rinse Tooter off in the stream of water cascading from the fountain.

"Did you decide which college you want to go to yet?" Vanessa prompted. She didn't mind hearing about this guy's love life, but the film was supposed to be about getting into college.

Nate frowned. "That's just the thing," he explained. "Yale. I want to go to Yale now." He shook his head and grinned unhappily down at the ground. "No way am I going to Brown. And the other schools' lax teams just aren't as good. But if I go to Yale and Blair doesn't get off the wait-list . . ." He leaned back on his elbows and squinted up at the sky. "I know she was the one who said it, but I guess I believed it, too—that we'd always wind up married." He sat up again, took off his frayed maroon St. Jude's baseball cap and rubbed his eyes tiredly. "Now I don't know."

Tiphany carried Tooter over to Vanessa and pressed his cold, wet body against the back of her neck.

"Eee!" Vanessa screamed, nearly dropping her camera. Then she and Tiphany burst into a fit of hysterical cackling.

Nate stood up, still deep in thought as he ambled away.

Over on his park bench Dan tossed his ice cream in the trash and lit a cigarette. It was weird, but he and Nate were almost thinking the same thing. He'd always thought he and Vanessa would be together forever. Now he wasn't so sure.

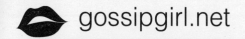
gossipgirl.net

Disclaimer: All the real names of places, people, and events have been altered or abbreviated to protect the innocent. Namely, me.

hey people!

Glinda the good witch

Okay, so everyone wants a fairy godmother. Well, a young buxom girl who hails from the Upper West Side and may or may not make the most embarrassing mistakes of her life on a weekly basis just happens to have one in the form of a tall, blond, beautiful senior. As we all know, **S** is the master of turning infamy into magic. Don't look now, but **J** could just be the next Jessica Simpson! Or better yet, the next **S** . . .

Strange company

One of the reasons most of us can't wait to go to college next year, no matter where we got in, is because we get to live on our *own*—without parents or nannies or housekeepers or bodyguards or *anyone* watching over us. Even if some of us have our own wings or floors, or even our own kitchens or whatever at home, the point is, we want *out*. Unless, that is, you're *already* out of the house—like someone we know—and it's not working out because of certain uninvited guests . . .

The truth about Liberty or Lolita or whatever she's calling herself these days

I'll tell you what I heard. That ferret-toting girl with the oddly braided purple-and-black hair? She used to be a nice girl. By that I mean she went to a good private girls' school on the Upper East Side, lived in a town house, and played tennis. Senior year she decided to rebel, "forgot" to apply to college, dropped out of school, got disowned from her family, and started wandering the country giving piercings to make money. Whenever she runs out of cash, she always comes back to town to mooch off her old friends and steal their clothes. And she's always so cheerful about it all, it usually takes a while for people to catch on.

Your e-mail

Dear GG,
I'm the chief of obstetrics and gynecology at Lenox Hill Hospital in the birth-and-delivery unit. I happened to be on the premises when a laboring woman was rushed in, escorted by her teenage daughter. Only minutes later I was called away on another emergency, but I was so impressed with the way the daughter was coaching her mother, I wanted to find out her name so I could recommend her to Yale's premed program, which is where I went. The mother was registered under the name Rose, but I can't find the daughter anywhere. Can you help?
—drpepper

Dear drpepper,
I think someone's day—no, *life*—is about to be made.
—GG

Dear GG,
Don't you think it's kind of rude to, like, join a really exclusive sisterhood that really means something to the other members, and then, like, totally never even call the people or anything again? I mean, why join in the first place?
—myowngrl

Dear myowngrl,
Didn't you ever do anything you regretted?
—GG

Sightings

B walking through **Sheep Meadow** wearing a **Burberry** print **Snugli**, her new baby sister all tucked up inside. Looks like **B**'s discovered her soft and furry side. **S** and a very famous fashion photographer choosing apparel in **Jeffrey** for a shoot. There was a certain crystal-studded bustier that **S** simply does not have the goods for. Either she's planning on getting implants, they're using falsies, or the bustier's for another girl. . . . **N** checking out the sterling silver baby gifts in **Tiffany & Co.** He can buy me a rattle anytime. **V** and that black-and-purple-haired girl in a conga line with **C** and his monkey at the **Five and Dime** in **Williamsburg**. No comment. And where was **D**? No comment.

Only one more day till the weekend, and I'm already hearing rumors about a party.

You know you love me,

gossip girl

show-and-tell

"This is Yale in the baby blanket I got her at Hermès. And this is her and Kitty Minky watching *Breakfast at Tiffany's* with me in the rocking chair. See, she even has on kitten socks with tiny ears and whiskers!"

Friday senior homeroom was the sacred half hour during which the Constance Billard seniors sat on the floor in the senior lounge—a tiny, empty fifth-floor classroom—drinking cappuccinos, trading gossip, and exchanging personal opinions about their new clothing purchases. This Friday was Blair's first day back at school since The Baby, so the half hour was given over to show-and-tell.

"And here she is sleeping in her little Moses basket."

"*Aw*," thirty girls chorused together.

"And where did she get that fantastic silver cow-jumping-over-the-moon mobile?" Laura Salmon demanded.

"It's from Tiffany. It was a gift."

From Nate, Serena added silently from where she sat on the outer edge of the group. Nate had even called her from Tiffany so she could help him pick something out.

"The basket she's sleeping in is so precious," added Isabel Coates. "I love the way the pink ribbon is woven into the handles."

Thanks, Serena thought to herself. She'd ordered the basket from a baby boutique in southern France and had it flown over especially. "It was hand woven by Alsatian monks from the branches of willow trees," Serena blurted out. "It's supposed to stay in the family and become an heirloom."

Meaning that it was a gift to Blair, too.

Blair looked up from her digital camera. She and Serena hadn't spoken since their unfortunate college-acceptance-letter-opening party, and it was pretty obvious that the generous baby gifts Serena and Nate had sent to her mom were meant as peace offerings. But Blair had never been one to forgive and forget easily.

The first bell rang and the tightly packed group of girls moaned and began to dissipate, collecting their books and pens and gum and hairbrushes and whatever else they'd need to make it through the day, while still hanging around to listen to Serena and Blair face off.

Serena stayed where she was, hugging her knees and watching Blair rearrange her school stuff in her too-small-for-books baby blue Fendi backpack. "She's beautiful," Serena told Blair earnestly.

Blair allowed her a smug half-smile. Yes, Yale *was* beautiful. "How'd last weekend go?" she demanded. "Where do you think you want to go?"

It was a trick question. If Serena said Yale, Blair would shoot fire out of her eyeballs and burn her to the ground. If she said another school, she'd be lying, since she still hadn't made up her mind. But Yale was closest to the city, and it had Lars and the Whiffenpoofs, and that uptight New Englandness that reminded her of home. Plus, how much fun would it be if she and Nate and Blair were friends again and all went there together?

She scooted her butt across the plush red carpet towards Blair and began to explain.

"Actually I fell in love. With all of them. Every school." She blushed as she tucked a loose strand of hair behind her ear. "I fell in love with my tour guides. They were all boys and they were so—"

Blair held up her hand and rolled her eyes. Did anyone or anything ever change? "I don't want to know." Actually, she did, but she knew Serena would eventually tell her anyway.

"And what about you?" Serena asked curiously. "How'd it go at Georgetown?"

Blair rolled her eyes again and touched her hair self-consciously. "You don't want to know."

Serena shrugged her shoulders. "It doesn't matter. You're going to get into Yale anyway," she stated confidently.

The second bell rang but the other girls dawdled, watching Serena and Blair out of the corners of their eyes as they pretended to drink out of empty cappuccino cups.

"I heard Serena got a huge modeling contract for next year so she's going to give Blair her spot at Yale. Blair just has to pretend to be her," Kati Farkas whispered to Isabel Coates.

And who will Serena pretend to be? Kate Moss?

"I heard she and Blair are going to take their babies to Yale with them and start a lesbos-with-babies support group," Isabel hissed back.

"Oh my God. I totally saw Serena at my mom's gyno yesterday," Laura Salmon volunteered. "I'm waiting for my mom, and then I hear Serena telling him how she'd gotten all these diseases from the guys she slept with this weekend. Ew!"

"Wait, I thought they were fighting," Kati pointed out. "Look, they're hugging."

Each girl turned to gape over her shoulder as Serena and

Blair took hold of each other. "Nate's been calling, like, ten times a day every day to ask about you," Serena murmured as she pressed her cheek against Blair's.

Blair bit her lower lip. "He sent Yale some really cute stuff."

"You know he loves you," Serena said, even though she didn't need to. "And we're all so much happier when we're not fighting."

"Yeah," Blair admitted. But Nate was going to have to prove it to her on his own.

Not that she'd be that hard to win over.

glinda the good witch and
her munchkin helper

"Can I sit here?" Elise asked Jenny at lunchtime on Friday.

"I don't know why you'd want to," Jenny grumbled. Ever since her ghastly picture had appeared in that magazine, she'd been creeping around with her head down, avoiding public places at all costs. Just being in school at all was excruciating. But her father had forced her to go, and now she was parked at her usual beside-the-mirror table, glaring at her reflection.

"I brought you an ice cream sandwich." Elise sat down across from her and pushed the ice cream toward Jenny.

Jenny pushed it away. She was on a food strike. "I'm not hungry. Actually, I was about to leave," she added grouchily. So Elise was making an effort to be friends again? Honestly—she wasn't in the mood.

Elise drizzled honey from a plastic packet into a teacup, beginning the little tea ceremony she'd had with herself every day at lunchtime since she and Jenny started fighting. "Just sit with me a little while," she begged in a voice verging on desperate.

Jenny knitted her eyebrows together. "Why should I?"

Elise stirred her tea and took a careful sip. "I don't know." She glanced around the room, as if looking for someone. "Because I asked you to?"

Jenny sighed heavily and stood up. "Look, I'm going up to the computer lab, okay?" At least up there she could hide from everyone's vicious stares while she pretended to send e-mails to all the friends she didn't have. "See you later."

Elise grabbed her arm. "Wait. Sit down. Just one more minute."

Jenny pulled her arm away. "What's your problem?"

Elise's freckled face turned beet red. "I just—" Then Serena plunked her beautiful ass down at their table and Elise let out a huge sigh of relief. "I thought I was going to have to sit on her to keep her down here," she grumbled.

"What's going on?" Jenny demanded. So now Elise and Serena were, like, working *together* to sabotage her life even worse than it had already been sabotaged? That was just peachy.

Serena pulled a stack of magazines from out of her bag. "Before you say anything, can I just show you the stuff Jonathan Joyce has done?" She rifled through the magazines and started pointing out pictures. "There. And there. And how cool is this?"

Jenny stared glassy-eyed at the photos. Models frolicking on a bed wearing little or no makeup, old T-shirts, and baggy men's trousers. A girl with her legs tucked up underneath her, drinking a glass of milk. A man kissing his dog. A stewardess asleep in an airport lounge with a pilot's coat draped over her. There was nothing provocative about the pictures. They were just plain good.

"He wants to shoot us on the merry-go-round in Central Park on Saturday," Serena continued. "The clothes are awesome—Jonathan's already got a whole rack of stuff he and I picked out together." She beamed at Jenny. "And the best part is, whatever we wear on the shoot, we get to keep."

Jenny didn't know what to say. Sure, it sounded exciting,

and the keeping-the-clothes thing was definitely a plus, but how did she know it wasn't just another degrading look-at-the-girl-with-the-big-boobs stunt?

"I have a birthday party to go to in Williamsburg on Saturday," she protested lamely.

"But that's not till nighttime," Elise countered. "I could come with you to the shoot, and I could shout or blow a whistle if I think your integrity is being compromised."

Leave it to Elise to put it into the type of clinical terms she'd read in one of her mom's self-help books. Jenny crossed her arms over the part of her integrity that was most often compromised.

"I made him promise not to shoot us in anything too revealing," Serena added. "He's really only interested in our faces anyway."

Jenny examined her reflection in the mirrored wall in front of her. She had a good face, and this famous guy wanted to take a picture of it. What was the big deal?

She took a deep breath. "Okay. I'll do it."

"Yippee!" Serena hugged her tightly. "It's going to be awesome, you'll see!"

The other girls eating in the lunchroom looked on curiously. "Maybe Jenny's agreed to donate the fat tissue from her boobs for Serena's implants," Mary Goldberg hazarded.

Or maybe Serena had found the perfect way to avoid the gang of Ivy League suitors coming to the city to see her on Saturday!

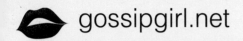
gossipgirl.net

Disclaimer: All the real names of places, people, and events have been altered or abbreviated to protect the innocent. Namely, me.

hey people!

What's this about a party?

So it's in Brooklyn and the people throwing it are basically not the type of people we see socially, but there's not much else going on this weekend, and a party isn't made by the people who throw it: it's made by the people who go. So I say, let's go, and get everyone we know to go, and make it rock. You dig?

Your e-mail

Q: Dear GG,
I go to Georgetown and I heard that so many people used Georgetown as their safety this year that the school is doing all this stuff to get people to come there. Like they're sending this group of girls up to New York this weekend to recruit all the kids that got in.
—gshock

A: Dear gshock,
Does this particular group of girls happen to have dyed blond hair and shaving scars on their legs?
—GG

Q: Dear GG,
I am in the ROTC program at Yale, which means my tenure here is sponsored by the army, and I'm in basic training at the same time. The officer in charge of my program got a letter from this girl who said she was wait-listed at Yale, but she would join the

program if they promised her a spot. So the program officer decides to send me down to NYC to meet her. She wrote on this weird stationery with shoes all over it and put a picture of her baby sister in the letter. Her baby sister's name is Yale. Sounds like a nutjob, huh?
—armygurl

Dear armygurl,
You don't know what you're in for. My advice: Wear your helmet.
—GG

Sightings

N in **FAO Schwarz**, trying to decide between a life-size stuffed horse and a crib entertainment center that plays DVDs and MP3s. It's nice that he's so generous and all, but this is getting ridiculous. **S** and **J** in Bendel's, shopping to their hearts' content while **J**'s friend **E** dutifully schlepped the bags. **B** introducing her new baby sister to **Barneys'** shoe department, where everybody knows her name. Ten handsome boys on the New Haven line singing a song from *West Side Story*. That ferret-toting friend of **V**'s buying a duffel bag full of booze in a **Williamsburg** liquor store. Guess someone's getting ready to party hardy? **D** sitting alone in a Williamsburg diner late at night, writing. A birthday poem for **V**, perhaps?

Don't forget, and don't forget to tell everyone you know not to forget—tomorrow night is all about behaving badly in Brooklyn.

See you there!

You know you love me,

gossip girl

and he didn't think anyone would come

"Happy birthday." Dan handed Vanessa the poem he'd written for her and leaned against the door frame. "I wanted to give you this before anyone gets here."

"Don't say, '*If* anyone is coming,'" Vanessa warned. "They'll come." She leaned over the bathroom sink, squinting at her reflection as she applied Tiphany's purpley-black lipstick to her lips. Then she sat down on the toilet and began to read the poem out loud.

> *a list of things you love:*
> *black*
> *steel-toed boots*
> *dead pigeons*
> *dirty rain*
> *irony*
> *me*
>
> *a list of things I love:*
> *cigarettes*
> *coffee*
> *you and your apple-white arms*

but the thing about lists is
they tend to get lost

"Thanks," Vanessa said. She folded the piece of paper and tucked it into the drawer in the vanity under the sink where Ruby kept all her hair goop and makeup.

It was kind of a weird response to a poem that was supposed to be bittersweet.

"Jesus, dude, you need to start taking happy pills," Tiphany muttered from out in the hall. "How can you write your girlfriend a birthday poem that sounds so *melancholy*?" She nudged Dan out of the way, grabbed the tube of lipstick from off the sink, and smeared some on her lips. "Roses are red, violets are blue." She pulled Vanessa upright and kissed her on the cheek, leaving a smudgy, purpley-black imprint. Then she kissed her on the other cheek. "Babe, you look hot with lips all over you!"

The two girls giggled and checked each other out in the mirror. Tiphany was wearing a black silk camisole borrowed from Ruby's closet. "Nice shirt," Vanessa noted.

"Nice pants," Tiphany said back. Vanessa had borrowed Ruby's zebra-striped pajama bottoms and they actually kind of worked with a black denim miniskirt, a black T-shirt, and combat boots. Very Blondie meets the Sex Pistols.

Dan wandered away, wishing Tiphany hadn't been her usual rude self and eavesdropped on his poem. So what if it wasn't all happy and cheerful and fun? It was still a love poem. And there was a message in it, if only Vanessa had taken the time to listen.

"I was thinking tonight might be a good night for a little piercing," Tiphany announced.

Vanessa glanced at her in the mirror. Tiphany's ears weren't even pierced. "Really? Like where?"

Tiphany grinned and wiggled her eyebrows ominously. "Not me, silly. You!"

The downstairs buzzer rang repeatedly and Tiphany grabbed Vanessa's arm and tugged her out of the bathroom. "I invited some people. You don't mind, do you?"

"Of course not," Vanessa said, glad to get away from the topic of piercing.

Dan buzzed them in and a moment later a troop of enormous guys in dusty, paint-smeared coveralls stomped into the apartment in their work boots.

"Hey boys." Tiphany dragged her army-issue duffel bag across the living room and opened it up. It was full of pint bottles of Grey Goose vodka. "This is my construction team. They don't speak much English." She handed each guy a bottle and then cracked one open herself. "Time to get happy!"

Dan went into the kitchen to make himself a cup of bad coffee. The construction guys smelled like paint thinner and were probably all psychopaths, just like Tiphany. But if they didn't speak English, he wouldn't have to talk to them, which was a good thing.

Vanessa didn't mind a bunch of strange guys in her house as long as they behaved themselves. At least now it felt more like a party. She went over to the stereo and put on Ruby's band's EP. Because it was her birthday she kind of missed her sister.

"*'Prick my finger, kiss my ass!'*" Ruby's voice howled from out of the speakers.

"*Serena! I just met a girl named Serena!*" a more melodic group of voices echoed from outside the apartment.

The front door was still open. Out in the hall stood a boyish blond boy followed by nine other guys, all wearing navy blue suits and Yale ties, with red roses in their buttonholes.

"Is Serena here yet?" the blond boy asked. Actually, he didn't ask the question so much as *sing* it.

"*Noooot yeeeet,*" Tiphany sang back. *"But cooommmme ooonnn innnnn!"* She handed each boy a bottle of Grey Goose. "Do you guys dance, too, or just sing?"

Dan stood in the kitchen, chain-smoking and gulping coffee. The party was turning into something out of *West Side Story*—the construction workers versus the singers. Maybe there'd even be a rumble.

Vanessa perched on the windowsill, filming people. The party was already so random, she couldn't imagine what would happen next.

Then the front door edged open a crack and a white monkey wearing a little red monogrammed *S* T-shirt scampered in.

"Sweetie!" Tiphany cried, scooping the monkey up in her arms. "Tooter's asleep in the closet. But if he knew you were here, I bet he'd come out and play."

"Anyone want a cigar?" Chuck Bass asked, brandishing a handful of them. "My dad's footman just brought back a whole suitcaseful from Cuba."

His footman?

The Whiffenpoofs and Tiphany's construction team helped themselves to cigars. Tiphany carried Chuck's monkey over to the closet where Tooter was sleeping on the floor, curled up on top of Dan's favorite gray sweater. "No monkey business in there, okay, kids?" she said, closing the door partway to give them some privacy. She turned to Vanessa. "Now how 'bout that piercing?"

Vanessa smiled nervously. "I always kind of wanted one on my lip."

"Done!" Tiphany grabbed one of her burly construction guys by the shirt. "Ice, needles, vodka, matches. In the bathroom. Go," she ordered, pushing him away again.

Suddenly four blond girls wearing gray Georgetown sweatshirts appeared at the door, holding hands. "Is Blair Waldorf here yet?" one of them asked.

"Not yet," Tiphany replied, as if she'd known Blair all her life. She doled a bottle of vodka out to each girl. "But I'm giving piercings in the bathroom if you want to come."

The four girls glanced giddily at one another, their eyes shining. They'd always wanted matching tattoos. Matching navel pierces would be even better.

"Let's do it!" they cried unison.

Vanessa put down her camera and followed them down the hall to the bathroom. After all, it was her birthday. Why shouldn't she?

Because it was going to hurt like hell?

b & n

Yale had a full-time baby-nurse who was sharing Myrtle's room, but whenever Blair heard the baby fuss, she'd dash into the room before the baby-nurse even got there and stroke Yale's bald head until she settled down again. She'd been doing it so regularly, the baby-nurse didn't even bother to get up when she heard Yale cry through the baby monitor, for soon enough she'd hear Blair croon, "Who's my little princess?" in a voice no one knew Blair was capable of.

Tonight, though, the baby-nurse would actually have to do her job, because Blair was going out.

"I'll be back in two hours," she promised her tiny sister.

The cab let her off on a scrap of Broadway in Williamsburg that could only be described as miserable. Garbage was strewn all over the sidewalk and every doorway was scrawled with graffiti. She supposed that shaven-headed freak Vanessa and her sister thought it was urban and tough and cool to live in a place like this, but Blair could live without urban and tough and cool, thank you very much. Fifth Avenue suited her just fine.

She mounted the pigeon-shit-spattered cement slab that served as a step and buzzed up to Vanessa's apartment. No answer. She buzzed again. Again, no answer. Now what was she supposed to do?

"I think they left it open," said a familiar voice.

Blair whipped around to find Nate standing below her on the sidewalk. There they were, together, in Brooklyn. It was most unexpected.

As if he wasn't the reason she'd come to the party in the first place.

"I only came by to see who was here. I can't stay for long," she told him hastily. Nate looked kind of tired and unkempt, but in a cute way. Like he'd taken a nap in his clothes. Actually, he looked exactly the way she felt.

"Me too," he said, shyly checking her out with those glittering green eyes of his. "You look pretty. I—I like your hair."

Blair touched her hair. He was the only person in the entire universe who'd noticed that it was slightly darker than before. "Thanks."

"So how's everything at home with the baby and all?" Nate asked. He shoved his hands in his pockets as though he wasn't sure what to do with them.

Someone threw a bottle of vodka out of an upstairs window and it splintered on the sidewalk only twenty feet away. Blair stepped down off the cement slab. She wasn't going upstairs, not now.

"Yale is . . ." Her voice trailed off as she struggled to find the right words to describe her little sister. *"Perfect,"* she said finally.

There was a happy sheen in Blair's eyes that hadn't been there before. "I'd really like to meet her sometime," Nate added.

Blair reached for his arm. What were they doing at a party in Brooklyn that neither of them wanted to go to? "Let's go *now*."

Just then a taxi pulled up and Serena, Jenny, Elise, and two guys dressed in matching banana yellow Dolce & Gabbana suits stepped out. Then another cab pulled up and out came four models in Carmen Miranda outfits complete with fruit bowl headdresses. Then another cabload of models, and then the Raves—yes, the entire band, minus the lead singer, who had just quit—pulled up in yet another cab.

"Our Hummer limo broke down so we had to get cabs," Jenny explained to Blair and Nate with a happy giggle.

Blair tightened her grip on Nate's arm and pulled him toward the first empty taxi. "Come on."

Serena winked as they climbed into the backseat. "Be good, you two!"

Blair smiled and let her head fall back against the cab's fake-leather upholstery. Nate's leg was touching hers and her whole body was burning with the warmth of it. She felt kind of like Sandy at the end of the original *Grease* movie, when she and Danny ride off into the sky in that souped-up car, leaving everyone else at the school carnival. It was always pretty obvious to Blair what Sandy and Danny were about to do next, what with Sandy wearing those black vinyl hot pants and everything. He couldn't keep his hands off her.

"You're the one that I want—ooh, ooh, ooh, honey!"

Nate slipped his hand between Blair's knees and left it there.

Oh, she'd be good all right.

j travels with an entourage

Dan hardly recognized his sister. She and Serena burst into the party looking like movie stars in matching turquoise-and-black-striped leggings, white pointy ankle boots, and turquoise leather vests. Their hair was blown out, they had on fake eyelashes, and their lips were smeared with hot pink lipstick.

Very eighties biker bitch meets the Mod Squad.

Better still, they were followed by a whole crew of models and fashion people from their photo shoot, and the members of a very hot new band called the Raves. Elise was there, too, wearing the bright orange jumpsuit that Jonathan Joyce had given her as a gift for being such a doll on the shoot.

Jenny sashayed up to Dan and kissed him on the cheek. "Happy birthday!" she squealed, even though she knew perfectly well it wasn't his birthday. She'd had the time of her life today and she was brimming with adrenaline. "Where's Vanessa?"

Dan tucked his ninetieth cigarette of the evening between his lips and lit it quickly. "In the bathroom, getting pierced," he answered bitterly.

"Wow!" Jenny kissed him on the cheek again. "What a great party!"

The band began to set up their equipment in the living room. Elise came over to drag Jenny away. "If you'll excuse us, Daniel, there's something I'd like to show Jennifer." She grabbed Jenny's elbow. "You've got to see this. It's in the closet."

Would that be two little animals making fuzzy whoopee, perhaps?

Dan didn't know what he'd been so worried about. Jenny was fine. Maybe that was the difference between fourteen and eighteen. When you were fourteen, something that seemed like the end of the world today could be completely forgotten tomorrow. When you were eighteen, your life was that much closer to being over.

Oh, please. He's not even eighteen yet!

The band began to play and immediately people started throwing their bodies around. In the last hour a steady stream of people had trickled in and the apartment was packed with kids from every private school in Manhattan. Now that they were second-semester seniors, it didn't matter whether they knew Vanessa or not. Give them a reason to get crazy and people would turn up.

Dan didn't much feel like dancing or getting crazy. Instead he decided to get drunk. Wandering into the living room, he grabbed a bottle of Grey Goose from Tiphany's half-empty sack and then hunkered by the wall to drink and watch the band play. Chuck Bass was dancing with one of the girls from Georgetown. The girl's newly pierced navel was covered with a Band-Aid and the metal whistle hanging from a chain around her neck kept bobbing up and slapping her in her seriously pugged nose.

Considering her dance partner, that whistle just might come in handy.

A girl in army fatigues, complete with helmet and dog tags, walked up to Dan and saluted. "Have you seen Blair Waldorf?" she asked.

Dan shook his head and took a giant swig of vodka. He wasn't exactly sure how it would manifest itself, but his own brand of craziness was not far off.

s can't keep her boys straight

Serena danced with the two gay stylists from the shoot, their banana yellow suits clashing with her turquoise-and-black leggings in a garish eighties way she just couldn't get enough of.

"Serena?" A tall boy with silver-rimmed spectacles bobbed into her line of vision and took her hand. Serena stopped dancing, her heart all aflutter. It was Drew, from Harvard. Or was it Brown?

"Hi," she said slowly, batting her fake eyelashes at him. She pointed at her crazy striped leggings and pointy white boots. "You see, this is the way I normally dress." She was struggling now to place Drew. Already the boys had blurred together. Was he the xylophone player or the painter?

Drew smiled tightly. He looked sort of uncomfortable in his neatly pressed J. Crew ensemble and brown suede shoes. It was as if he couldn't wait for her to say, Let's blow this joint and go have an intimate cup of coffee someplace nice and quiet.

Serena hesitated. She wanted to be that girl, she really did. The girl who drank coffee with her boyfriend. A couple. But she didn't want it badly enough to miss the party.

All of a sudden someone grabbed her around the waist and lowered her into an exaggerated dip. Serena's breath caught in her throat as she gazed up into the square-jawed-jock face of Drew's meathead roommate. "Whoa!" she exclaimed, her eyes wide.

"You remember Wade," Drew said, looking even more uncomfortable than he had before. "He insisted on coming."

Wade pulled her close and kissed her on the lips. *Smack!* "Aren't you glad?" he demanded.

Serena didn't want to appear easy, but she had to admit that she *was* glad. The more the merrier, as far as she was concerned. A petite strawberry blond woman with a tidy black Kate Spade purse tapped her on the shoulder. "Do you know Nate Archibald?" the woman asked.

Serena nodded. "He already left." Drew was still standing next to her, hands in his pockets, looking as if he needed something to do. "This is my friend Drew," Serena told the strawberry blond woman. "He goes to—"

"Harvard," Drew said, holding out his hand in that geekily charming way of his.

On the other side of the room the Whiffenpoofs began singing backup for the Raves. They sounded fantastic. Serena stood on tiptoe to wave at them and all ten boys blew her a kiss. But wasn't there somebody missing? The artist from Brown. Didn't he love her as much as the others?

Oh, did he ever.

People were huddled by the windows, looking out at something happening down on the street. "Put me on your shoulders?" she asked Wade sweetly.

Wade carried Serena over to the windows and she gazed over the tops of the onlookers' heads to see what all the fuss was about. Down on the street, someone was spray-painting a mural in shades of green and gold. It was Christian, his dark head bent seriously over his work. As the mural took shape it became apparent that it was a portrait of Serena, with fluorescent green butterflies in her hair and gold wings sprouting out of her shoulders, like some sort of glorious angel.

Serena giggled, embarrassed by Christian's gaudy adoration, but reveling in it just the same. Maybe it wasn't true love she wanted after all. Maybe it was just . . . *love*. And that was all around her.

b's teething rattle turns n on

"Walk on this side of the room," Blair whispered. "The floor-boards creak over there."

Nate followed her across the nursery, lit only by a paper moon nightlight, to where Yale lay sleeping in her white lace-covered bassinet. In the corner by the window, the life-size dappled gray pony he'd had sent over from FAO Schwarz stood watching them like a sentry.

The baby was swaddled in a pink blanket and was lying on her back, her face puckered and red and new-looking. "See how her eyes are moving underneath the lids," Blair whispered. "She's dreaming."

Nate couldn't imagine what somebody so new to the world could be dreaming about, but he supposed it must be kind of like one of those dreams he had when he was severely stoned. Nothing happened, he just *felt* stuff. And he always woke up hungry.

Blair reached into the bassinet and retrieved a little silver rattle. It looked like a tiny barbell. "This was mine when I was a baby." She turned it over. "See all the little bite marks?"

She handed the rattle to Nate. At first glance it appeared smooth, but when he looked closely he could see hundreds of indentations. It was no surprise that Blair had been a voracious teether, obsessive and aggressive right from the start. But there was something calm about her now, as if through soothing the baby she'd learned to soothe herself.

Nate handed the rattle back and it shook noisily. Instantly, Yale began to fuss and whimper, her arms and legs kicking out in all directions and her face puckering like a dried apricot.

Blair leaned over the bassinet and picked her sister up. "Shhh," she whispered. "It was nothing. Go back to sleep." She rocked back and forth until Yale stopped fussing. Then she put the baby down and tucked the blanket up around her. "There. Go to sleep," she said again, and then looked up at Nate.

"She's beautiful," he told her, his voice cracking. Silently he reached for Blair's hand and pulled her out into the hallway. She closed the nursery door and he hugged her fiercely, pressing his lips against hers. "My parents are out," he whispered into her hair.

The penthouse was so hushed, Blair could practically hear her own heart beating. Tyler and Aaron and were watching movies in the library, and her mom and Cyrus were out. But she couldn't exactly have sex with Nate while Yale lay sleeping innocently in the next room. She closed her eyes and kissed him again before whispering, "Okay, I'm ready."

Finally.

j looks forward to a scandalous future

Jenny had never been a big dancer, but how could she not dance in those crazy white pointy boots? And the amazing thing about her turquoise leather vest was it held everything in place. No boob whiplash. No accidental groping. No wiggly-wobbly. Even without the vest, though, she would have been okay. Better than okay.

The Raves stopped playing and announced that they were taking a short break. The Whiffenpoofs, however, were just getting going.

"One, two, a one, two, three—" they began to sing in their traditional a cappella harmony. *"Jenny, oh, Jennifer,"* they began to serenade her. *"Serena's little sister, Jennifer. They don't look alike. One's tall, one's short, but they're the craziest gals in any port."*

Serena came and draped her arm around Jenny's shoulders, swaying back and forth to the song. The other party-goers drifted back and forth across the room, not paying much attention now that the real music had cut out.

"Jennifer, she's got big huge bazongas!" Chuck Bass sang loudly as he staggered past the two girls, shaking his ass drunkenly with his monkey on his shoulders and his military school beret on his head. A few titters echoed throughout the room.

Uh-oh.

"You know they did it once, right?" a girl from Seaton Arms whispered to her friend. "Got caught at a party in October, in the *bathroom*. She was, like, totally naked and Chuck was giving it to her on the *toilet*."

"I thought he was gay," said a girl wearing a brand-new Vassar T-shirt.

"Everyone wants to squeeze Jenny's great big boobeez!" Chuck carried on obnoxiously.

"Chuck Bass has a hairy ass!" Serena countered loudly. "Just ignore him," she told Jenny.

But instead of turning purple with outrage and utter shame, Jenny couldn't stop giggling. Two weeks ago Chuck's little performance would have been devastating. Now everyone was laughing at him, not with him. And now that she'd been through a scandal—or two or three—and come out ahead, she was more resilient. She had a past, a history. She was the girl no one would be able to stop talking about. Big bazongas and all, she, Jennifer, was destined for success.

And if life took a crappy turn and things went irreparably wrong, she could always get sent to boarding school like her father had threatened. There she could reinvent herself. Maybe she'd even come back from boarding school and reinvent herself *again*, just like Serena had done.

She might even have as many boyfriends as Serena. One day.

d explores a new talent

"Could I borrow a smoke, bro?" Damian Polk, the lead guitarist of the Raves and one of Dan's musical favorites, asked him. Dan was too drunk to be starstruck. He held up the rumpled half-empty pack of Camels he'd opened only a half hour ago, then Damian lit his cigarette with Dan's yellow plastic Bic. Damian was wearing a sort of brown canvas military coat with words in Finnish or some other random language painted on it in black. It was the type of coat only a famous person could get away with. "Don't happen to know who lives here, do you?" he asked.

"*I* do," Dan responded drunkenly. "Sort of. With my girlfriend. It's her older sister's place, but she's away." He decided not to mention Tiphany. He preferred to think that Tiphany didn't exist. And now that he thought about it, he hadn't seen Tiphany or Vanessa all night. How long could a piercing take, he wondered, his head murky with vodka.

Damian nodded thoughtfully. "Any idea who wrote all those songs in those black leather books in the other room?"

Dan wondered suddenly if he hadn't passed out and was dreaming this entire conversation. "Poems," he corrected, blinking away the happy melodic notes of the Whiffenpoofs, who were still serenading his sister. A tall guy with wire-rimmed glasses and a short woman with strawberry blond hair tangoed across the floor. "Those are my *poems*." He tried to stand up but his ankles buckled and he slumped against the wall again. If he didn't move soon, he was going to piss himself.

Damian tucked his coat behind him and squatted down in front of Dan. "I'm telling you, man, they're *songs*."

Dan stared woodenly at the famous five-inch-long scar that cut across Damian's famous forehead. It was supposedly from a BMX bike accident. Was he brain damaged or something? "Dude," he insisted. "I wrote them. They're *poems*."

"Songs. Songs, songs, songs." Damian held out his hand and coaxed Dan into a standing position. "Come on, I'll show you."

Dan stumbled along after Damian, bumping into people and slurring his sorrys.

"When you guys gonna start playing again?" someone yelled.

"Soon, asshole," Damian muttered, giving them the finger.

Vanessa's room was just as crowded as the living room. The other members of the Raves were gathered on her bed, sorting through Dan's notebooks.

"Did you see this one? It's called 'Sluts,'" the bass player told Damian, holding up the poem. "It'd be the perfect, like, pissed-off love ballad, you know? Like the perfect middle song for a show. Especially after this funny one, 'Killing Tooter.'"

Dan stared at them. There was still a very good chance he was dreaming or had died after being stepped on by one of Tiphany's huge construction-worker friends.

Damian nudged him forward. "I found the guy who wrote them. He's good-looking enough to be a front man."

Dan swayed in front of the others. Front man?

"But can he sing?" the drummer asked, giving Dan the once-over and pulling on his weird, scary mustache. The Raves had a mixed-bag kind of style. Part cool older brother, part serial killer.

Sing?

Damian clapped Dan on the back. "You'll give it a try, won't you? They're your songs, after all. Sing 'em however you want to. We play pretty loud, so you'll feel like you're shouting." He patted Dan's back again. "Just make it sound good, yeah?"

"Yeah."

As he followed the band into the living room, Dan felt like his body was in the hands of some maniacal puppeteer with a very twisted sense of humor. Next thing he knew, he'd be taking his shirt off.

Well, he is the front man, after all.

The drummer whacked his drums a few times and a hush of anticipation fell over the room. "We'll do 'Killing Tooter' first, yeah?" he asked Dan.

Dan nodded. He barely knew the words, but he was so drunk anyway, it wasn't like he'd be enunciating.

The band broke into a frenetic, rhythmic, slamming beat with an undulating bass line. It was perfect for the poem, or song, or whatever the fuck anyone wanted to call it.

"'You hungry? I made you something! Die, Tooter, die!'" Dan screamed into the microphone. "'You tired? I'll put you to sleep! Die, Tooter, die!'"

"'Die, Tooter!'" The Whiffenpoofs crooned in support.

The room was packed and immediately people picked up on the craziness of the moment, slam dancing and taking their clothes off.

Dan ripped off his shirt. What the hell? He gave everyone

the finger. "'You want some more? Come and get it! Die, Tooter, die!'"

Okay, so maybe he was completely shit-faced, but this was still better than wallowing in self-pity and dust bunnies back in the corner.

And at least he knew now, after all these years, that he'd been writing twisted, morbid *songs*, not poems.

v gets a kick in the ass

"Yo, is there somebody named Vanessa in there?" a guy yelled from outside the bathroom.

"Yeah?" Vanessa called back, and opened the door a crack. For the last half hour she'd been bent over the bathroom sink, running her lip under cold water, but it was still bleeding.

The guy shoved the phone into her hand. He was shirtless, and had a tattoo of a snake on his chest. "Same bitch called like five hundred times. Doesn't she get we're trying to listen to music out here?"

Vanessa took the phone and cradled it between her chin and shoulder while Tiphany applied ice to her lip. "Hello?"

"Hey, it's your sister, remember me?" Ruby shouted on the other end of the line. "What the fuck is going on over there?"

"I'm having a party," Vanessa explained, although it hardly explained anything. Ruby knew perfectly well that, other than Dan, Vanessa had exactly zero friends.

"Oh, yes, Miss Birthday Girl? And who might be attending this party?"

Vanessa glanced at Tiphany. "Is that your sister?" Tiphany mouthed. Vanessa nodded, and Tiphany pressed a fistful of ice into her hand. "Catch you later." She kicked away the blood-soaked towels littering the bathroom floor, leaving the door open behind her as she left. The cacophony of music and shouting and the smell of smoke and vodka almost knocked Vanessa over.

"Is that the Raves—*live*? What, did MTV like hire you to film their video or something?" Ruby demanded.

"I'm not sure," Vanessa answered honestly. She knew the party had swelled tremendously since she'd disappeared into the bathroom, but she hadn't realized to what extent. "So anyway, Tiphany has been staying here."

"Tiphany who?"

"Tiphany. You gave her the key. She said you told her she could crash here for as long as she wanted. She's been sleeping on your bed."

Ruby was silent for a moment. "Wait, I think I know who you're talking about. She has a ferret, right? And she comes with this whole story about how she's traveled the world and done all these things and she just needs a place to crash for a while?"

Check.

"I can't believe she still has the key. Don't you remember the story about the girl who was, like, *squatting* in the apartment when I moved in? I finally got the landlord to get rid of her, and the whole time she acted like we were best friends."

That did kind of sound like Tiphany. "But she's not even from here," Vanessa faltered. "She's from all over. She's got *wanderlust*." It was one of Tiphany's favorite words, but boy did it sound idiotic when Vanessa said it.

"She's a fuckup," Ruby corrected. "And a user. I bet she hasn't paid for any food or anything since she's been there. Except maybe alcohol."

Vanessa didn't know what to say. It was true. She and Dan had basically been feeding Tiphany for over a week.

"Besides, we're not allowed to have pets in our building. That ferret could get us evicted. Kick her out, babe. Okay?"

Vanessa was on the verge of tears. How could she have been so stupid and let this girl she didn't even know take over her life? It was like *Poison Ivy*, that awful Drew Barrymore movie Vanessa was embarrassed to admit she'd rented, where bad girl Drew moves in with a nice innocent girl and totally ruins her life.

"I'll call you tomorrow, okay?" Ruby promised.

"Okay." Vanessa hung up. Her hands were shaking. She tossed the phone into the sink and stormed into the living room, forgetting all about her bleeding lip.

Christ.

The apartment was mobbed. Girls from Constance Billard and Seaton Arms and all the other schools Vanessa wished she had nothing to do with were slam dancing and gyrating their asses against the pelvises of boys from St. Jude's and Riverside Prep. The members of Tiphany's "construction team," who Vanessa now suspected were probably professional burglars or worse, were attacking the living room wall with Tiphany's pick-axe; Tiphany's ferret and Chuck Bass's monkey were chasing each other and humping on Ruby's futon; and Tiphany herself was parked in front of the TV, playing one of the films Vanessa had made a few months back for all to see. But where was Dan? Had she been ignoring him or was he ignoring her?

Pushing through the crowd, Vanessa lunged at Tiphany and yanked the remote out of her hand. "That's private!" she yelled, snapping the TV off. Little by little she could feel her old outraged, pissed-off self coming back . . . and it felt great. What made her even more angry was that Tiphany had stolen it away from her.

Atta girl.

Tiphany laughed her goofy, loud, ain't-we-just-the-bestest-friends laugh. "Dan's a boring poet, and a really bad actor." She pointed across the living room. "But mix them together and look what you get!"

Vanessa glared at her, and then turned to see what she was pointing at. She didn't know how she could have missed it. There was Dan, standing on top of an overturned milk crate, shirtless and sweaty, biting the microphone as he spat out the words to his poems, pretending they were songs. She turned away again. She'd deal with him later.

"That's my sister's shirt," she told Tiphany levelly. "Put it back."

Tiphany's mouth opened slightly. "You're wearing her pants."

"She's *my* sister. Give it back," Vanessa ordered. "And then find your friends and your goddamned ferret and get the fuck out of here."

The rage that had been building since her conversation with Ruby in the bathroom suddenly consumed her. It was her birthday and no one seemed to give a flying fuck that they were trashing her house. She didn't even know most of these people. "Fuck everybody!" she shouted. "I want you all fucking *out*!!"

Of course no one could hear her, not over the din of Dan's drunken howl.

Vanessa had one thing going for her, though. It was her

apartment and she knew where the fuse box was. Shoving her way past a half-naked sweaty boy and his teetering-drunk girlfriend, she tore into the kitchen, climbed up on the counter, and opened the metal box above the stove. With a flick of a few switches, the music went dead and the only light left on was the one above her head.

"EVERYBODY OUT!" she shouted again, her mouth opening inhumanly wide, like Lucy on *Peanuts* when she's seriously pissed off at Charlie Brown, which hurt like hell with such a newly pierced lip.

"What the fuck?" a guy wearing nothing but a pair of orange Princeton boxer shorts demanded.

"Who the hell is she?" his girlfriend whined.

But these were well-bred kids, and no one likes to stick around at a party when they're not welcome. Slowly, people began to trickle out the door and down the stairs. Vanessa even thought she heard the distinct sound of a pick-axe clattering to the floor.

She sat down on top of the stove, swinging her combat boots against the oven door as she watched everyone leave.

"Why didn't she just ask us to keep it down or something?" somebody grumbled.

"What are we supposed to do now? It's only midnight," someone else complained.

Of course Chuck Bass had the perfect solution. "We'll move the party to my house!!" he cried, gathering up his monkey and tucking it into his shirt. He put his arm around two of the blond Georgetown girls. "You can even sleep over if you want."

Tiphany stalked past the kitchen wearing only a black bra, which was probably Ruby's too. She tossed something at Vanessa. "There's her goddamned shirt."

Vanessa didn't think that sort of behavior warranted a response. She watched with smug satisfaction as Tiphany grabbed her ferret by the scruff of the neck and dragged her army duffel bag across the living room and out the door.

It wasn't like she'd be homeless. Chuck had plenty of room.

d and *v* do it with words

There were only a few stragglers left now. Vanessa turned the fuses back on and surveyed the damage. She would have to hire a cleaning service to help her deal with it. Maybe she could find some way to charge it to Tiphany.

Dan was on his hands and knees, looking for his shirt and shoes. His scraggly brown hair was matted over his eyes and he could barely see.

Vanessa hopped off the stove. "You can stay," she told him gently. What had happened was her fault, after all. If she hadn't been so swept up in Tiphany's bullshit, she and Dan would be living together and getting along fine instead of drowning in disaster.

Dan found one Puma sneaker and shoved it on. One was better than none. He stood up. Vanessa's upper lip was crusty with blood but she still looked better than he felt.

"Gotta catch up with the band. They want me to be their front man," he slurred with drunken urgency.

Vanessa had no idea what he was talking about. Maybe if they just sat down and talked to each other like they always used to, things would go back to normal.

"It's my birthday," she reminded him, trying to keep her voice from breaking. "Will you read me the poem you wrote for me?"

Dan shook his head. Nearly everything he'd ever written was for Vanessa. "It's a song. They're all songs."

"Whatever." Vanessa retrieved the piece of paper from the bathroom drawer, grateful that some nosy girl hadn't rummaged around in there for some hair gel or something and taken the poem with her.

She handed it to Dan and sat down in front of him. It was such a relief just to be alone together again, even if the walls were crumbling down around them.

Dan's heart was still pumping wildly, but the rest of his body had slowed way down. He read the poem carefully, his tongue heavy with liquor and fatigue.

> *a list of things you love:*
> *black*
> *steel-toed boots*
> *dead pigeons*
> *dirty rain*
> *irony*
> *me*
>
> *a list of things I love:*
> *cigarettes*
> *coffee*
> *you and your apple-white arms*
>
> *but the thing about lists is*
> *they tend to get lost*

"They are lyrics, aren't they?" Dan observed. "I mean, that would be so much better with music." He tried to reread the poem again to himself, but the words began to dance around the page and he couldn't make sense of them anymore. He knew he'd written them for a reason, but he couldn't remember what the reason was.

Vanessa made a funny little gasping sound and he looked up to find her crying the gaspy, chokey sort of crying of someone who doesn't cry very often. Only a moment ago, Dan had been having a ball, shouting his lungs out into a microphone. How had everything gotten so serious all of a sudden?

Vanessa took his hand. Her face was wet and blotchy, her nose was running, and there was a bloody silver ring in her upper lip. "Look, I know everything is all messed up, but it's still gonna be okay. I mean, it's just like in your poem. I like ugly things. We both like it when things aren't perfect, right?"

Dan's hand hung limply in hers. He knew what Vanessa was saying was important, but he couldn't concentrate. What he needed was a cigarette, and as far as he could remember he was all out. Or maybe his cigarettes were with his other shoe. "I need to find my shoe," he told her.

The tears kept falling. Vanessa gripped his hand tightly, desperate to finish what she'd started, to explain what she thought Dan's poem meant and how true she thought it was. "We don't have to go to the same school or even live together. We can just *be*." She wiped her nose on the back of her free hand. There were little spots of blood on her zebra-striped pants from her piercing. She rubbed at them angrily. "No matter what we do, we'll always sort of be together, right?"

Dan nodded. "Right," he agreed robotically. It wasn't that he didn't feel her pain, he just couldn't have such an intense conversation right now.

Vanessa's shoulders shook with a silent sob. She wiped her

nose again, leaned forward, and kissed him on the lips. Dan tried to kiss her back, but he was afraid of hurting her lip.

"All right." She let go of his hand and attempted a smile. "Get out of here. Go be a rock star or whatever."

Dan stared at her. She was letting him go?

Duh.

"Would you just leave already?!" Vanessa gave his chest a nudge as she fought back another round of sobs.

Dan scrambled to his feet. He could barely see the floor, it was so littered with cigarette butts, empty bottles, left-behind clothes, and destroyed crap. "I can come back tomorrow and help clean up," he offered lamely as he limped away through the mess.

Like tomorrow he was going to be all bright-eyed and bushy-tailed and ready to put on rubber gloves and mop up with the Mr. Clean?

b and *n* do it for real

"You still have this?" Blair pulled the moss-green cashmere V-neck she'd given Nate over a year ago off the back of his desk chair, where he'd left it the night before. She turned it inside out, checking to see if the tiny gold heart pendant she'd sewn inside one of the sleeves was still there. It was.

Nate stood in the middle of the room, watching her. He wanted to whip his clothes off, grab her, and throw her on the bed, but he knew from experience that Blair liked to do things her way, so he would have to try and wait.

Blair put the sweater down and ran her hand over the model sailboat on Nate's desk. Beside it was a picture of him and his buddies from St. Jude's, holding up the two big fish they'd caught on a fishing trip up in Maine. With his strong, tanned arms, broad white smile, golden brown hair, and glittering green eyes, Nate was the cutest of them all. Not that she hadn't always known that.

She didn't know what she was waiting for, and she wasn't stalling exactly. She just hadn't been alone with him in this perfect, intimate way in so long, she was relishing it. And the funny thing was, all the other times—and there had been many—that she'd thought they were about to have sex, she'd been nervous and fidgety and hadn't been able to stop talking. But not this time.

"Do you want to listen to some music or put a movie on or something?" Nate asked, wondering if he needed to enhance the mood. If only he had some candles or incense or something. Massage oil? Handcuffs?

Okay, let's not get carried away.

Blair walked over to the bookshelf and turned on the ridiculous globe lamp that Nate had had since he was five. Then she switched off the overhead light. Light from the globe mingled with the moonlight shining through the skylight overhead, casting the room in a soft blue glow.

"There." She kicked off her black Kate Spade flats. Her toes were painted dark red and looked sexy even to her. She grinned at Nate. "Come here."

He did as he was told, tucking his hands up under her shirt and helping her off with it while she practically tore his head off removing his. Her bra was filmy, white, and wireless, and when she unhooked it, it fell away like tissue paper to the floor.

Nate stood his ground. He'd gotten this far so many times before, it wouldn't have surprised him if Blair's mom knocked on the door and told them that she was actually having triplets and the other two babies were arriving just this minute.

Blair wrapped her arms around his neck and pressed her body into his. All the times she'd imagined doing it, she'd put herself and Nate in place of the actors in a love scene in some old movie. Audrey Hepburn and Gary Cooper in *Love in the Afternoon*. Kathleen Turner and William Hurt in *Body Heat*. But this was so much better, because it was real, and it felt so *nice*.

He couldn't stop kissing her. She guided his hand down to the waistband of her jeans and then reached for his. Okay, so maybe no one was going to knock on the door and the sky wasn't going to fall in. Maybe this time it was really going to happen.

She pulled him backwards onto the bed and they shimmied out of their pants and underwear. Then there was nothing left but them. They kissed again in every kissable spot, until it became obvious that certain measures needed to be taken. Nate fumbled in his bedside bureau drawer for a condom.

Now for the awkward part.

Only it wasn't awkward. Without a word, Blair took the condom, kissed her way down his body, and carefully rolled it on just as she rolled on one of Yale's delicate baby socks. There. All better.

Nate had forgotten what it was like being with Blair. How touching her wasn't a haunted-house experience, where he blindly had to guess where things were and what they were, and wound up bumping into walls. With Blair, he just *knew*. And everything seemed to fit just right.

Blair didn't even have to tell Nate to slow down. They were so in sync, all she had to do was close her eyes and wrap her arms around him, arch her back a little, and feel it happening.

Tada!

When it was over, they lay on their backs, holding hands and smiling up at the ceiling, because they knew that in a few minutes they could do it again. They could spend the rest of their lives doing it if they wanted to. Have food sent up to Nate's wing of the town house. Take their finals online.

"Maybe I won't even go to college," Nate mused. Why

should he, when there was so much pleasure to be had? He kissed her hand. "We could sail around the world together. Have adventures."

Blair closed her eyes and tried to imagine sailing around the world with Nate on the yacht he'd build especially for them.

"I'd wear a different Missoni bikini every day and have the best tan," she whispered out loud.

In her head the fantasy continued. Their bodies would be all strong and wiry from working on the yacht and from their diet of raw fish, seaweed, and champagne. At night they'd make love under the stars and in the morning they'd make love to the sound of the seagulls' caws. They'd have beautiful, tan, blond, green-eyed babies who swam like dolphins and never wore clothes. They'd stop in exotic ports, where the natives would dance for them and give them gifts of rare jewels and furs. Eventually, they'd amass such a collection of treasure, they'd be known around the world as the richest seafarers in the universe, and pirates would come after them to plunder their booty and steal their impossibly beautiful Ralph Lauren model–type children. By then, having nothing better to do with all those hours on the boat, she and Nate would have their black belts in karate, and they would fight off the pirates, sending them plunging to their deaths in the shark-infested seas. Then they would sail off into the moonlight, unharmed, and more in love than ever.

It could happen.

"Or maybe we'll both go to Yale," she said hopefully. Some doctor at her mom's hospital had left a note with her doorman today saying he wanted to write her a recommendation to Yale's premed program. She'd never considered becoming a doctor, but if it was going to get her into Yale, why not?

"I'll play lacrosse and major in geology," Nate murmured into her hair.

"Yes," Blair agreed dreamily.

Nate would excavate the Connecticut woods looking for rocks and wearing the beautiful Aran sweaters she'd knit for him during her lengthy premed lectures. All the female premed students would be in love with a brilliant young biologist who also happened to be Blair's advisor, but she would pay him no mind—she'd only have eyes for Nate.

"And we'll live together," she added aloud. In a ramshackle old Victorian house right near campus. They'd make hot cider on the wood stove and cook s'mores in the fireplace.

Nate grinned happily. "We'll get a Great Dane."

"No, *two* great Danes and two cats," Blair corrected. And they'd be so involved in their studies and making love on their antique bed in their creaky Victorian bedroom that they'd forget to cut their hair or buy new clothes and they'd look like hippies, but they'd still graduate magna cum laude.

"And we'll get married," he whispered.

"Yes." Blair squeezed his hand beneath the sheets.

They'd have a gigantic wedding in St. Patrick's Cathedral, and when they returned from their yearlong honeymoon in the south of France, they'd live in a Fifth Avenue penthouse overlooking the park. She'd be the surgeon general of New York, and he'd stay home with their four golden-haired, green-eyed children, building sailboats in the living room. And he'd always pack a Hershey's Kiss in her lunch to show that he loved her.

Blair turned over and rested her head on Nate's chest. The

possibilities were endless, but they didn't have to decide now. The only decision they had to make right now was whether to do it again, or wait a few minutes and *then* do it.

His heartbeat rang in her ears, an urgent, vibrant sound. She lifted her head and kissed him.

Why wait?

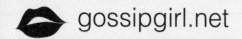 gossipgirl.net

topics ◀ **previous** **next** ▶ **post a question** **reply**

Disclaimer: All the real names of places, people, and events have been altered or abbreviated to protect the innocent. Namely, me.

hey people!

A movable feast

Last I checked, everyone was still breathing, barely. Would last night—which wound up carrying on until late this afternoon—count as one party or two? Were those really the Raves, or just some geeky Williamsburg bar band impersonating them? And was our own favorite Upper West Side poet really so drunk that he couldn't find his other shoe? Not that it affected his singing. He almost sounded better in Manhattan than he did in Brooklyn, but maybe that's because we were all so merry by then. My favorite part of the evening was when those blond girls with the matching Georgetown sweatshirts and the whistles and tummy Band-Aids did a little cheerleader cheer to the music and then invited all the guys into the bedroom to play spin-the-bottle. And I'd heard Georgetown girls were all so chaste.

Two notably missing persons remained missing throughout the evening, and are still reported missing. Word has it they are missing together and that for the remainder of the school year we will have to watch them being sappy together because love is a beautiful thing and blah, blah, blah. But I'm sure we can drum up a few surprises to make their lives more interesting—right?

Your e-mail

 Dear GG,
I'm just worried about my sister. She had a huge party in

Brooklyn last night and a lot of shit went down. Chances are you were there. Is she okay?
—rb

Dear rb,
She looked too pissed off when she kicked us all out to be permanently scarred. We girls are pretty resilient. Although her lip may take some time to heal, and she could definitely use some help with the cleanup.
—GG

Dear GG,
Okay, so we go all the way up to New York to recruit this girl to go to our school and then she totally disappears. THEN we wind up, like, almost breaking this pact that has basically been our mission in life for two years. It's all her fault, and we really don't want her to go to our school or be in our sisterhood anyway.
—becs

Dear becs,
I'm not sure what I can do to help you out at this point. You've still got each other—right?
—GG

Sightings

S hosting a small all-male brunch at her Fifth Avenue apartment. Last the staff checked, the table was set for fourteen. **J** and **D** signing autographs outside **MTV** studios. They may not be famous yet, but if you *act* famous, the world is your oyster. **V** putting up Roommate Wanted signs throughout **Williamsburg**. **C** and his black-and-purple-haired girl chum pushing their pets in a doll carriage through the **Central Park Zoo**. Looks like he's found the perfect nanny for his monkey while he's away at **West Point** next year. Missing persons: **B** and **N**. Last seen sprinting from her building on Seventy-second Street and Fifth to his town house on Eighty-second Street off Park around eleven-thirty last night.

My head is still spinning with visions of monkeys and ferrets and girls in turquoise leather vests, but I'm not too hungover to throw out more questions:

Are **D** and **V** still together, or is it a just-friends thing now? What kind of "roommate" is she looking for exactly?

Will **D** become an internationally famous rock god?

Will **B** finally get into Yale? Will she have to join the army or become a doctor to do it?

Will **B** and **N** and **S** all go to Yale together? Is that really a good idea?

Will **J** become a famous and untouchable supermodel or will she mess up again and have to go to boarding school to escape the burning stares of passersby?

Will **N** ever be unfaithful to **B** again? If so, will he consider doing it with me?

I know you're dying to find out. But first, please, go home and get some rest.

You know you love me,

The only thing harder than
getting in is staying in.

THE CLIQUE

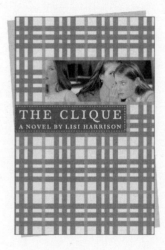 

Be sure to read both novels in the juicy
CLIQUE series, and keep your eye out for
Revenge of the Wannabes, coming May 2005.